THE SECRET OF THE GOLD JAGUAR

A Solve-the-Puzzles Adventure Tale

Alan Robbins

A PERIGEE BOOK

To Trudy, my fellow heuristist

Perigee Books
are published by
The Putnam Publishing Group
200 Madison Avenue
New York, NY 10016

Library of Congress Cataloging in Publication Data

Robbins, Alan.
The secret of the gold jaguar.

"A Perigree book."
Summary: An illustrated puzzle adventure focusing on the search for
an ancient idol hidden in the jungle of Central America.
1. Literary recreations — Juvenile literature.
2. Puzzles — Juvenile literature. [1. Literary recreations. 2. Puzzles.
3. Adventure and adventurers — Fiction] I. Title.
GV1493.R68   1985   793.73   84-18344
ISBN 0-399-51116-4

PRINTED IN THE UNITED STATES OF AMERICA
1   2   3   4   5   6   7   8   9   10

YOU are about to embark on a great adventure. Somewhere hidden in the dense jungles of Central America is an ancient idol in the shape of a jaguar. A mysterious organization has asked for help in finding this priceless relic.

YOU will have to solve the riddles of the Kryptec Indians, the forgotten tribe who worship the jaguar. YOU will have to find your way through the Lost City, an ancient maze whose corridors and byways challenge your every step. YOU will have to choose which of the four guardian temples to explore, trying to find the secret passage that leads to the jaguar's hidden lair.

Yes, there are difficult decisions ahead, tricky problems to solve and strange codes to break . . . *But you must press on!* There is no turning back now! Only sharp wits, scissors and a pencil stand between YOU and the secret of the Gold Jaguar.

How to Use This Book

The Secret of the Gold Jaguar is no ordinary adventure tale. Sure it's exciting, mysterious and intriguing—but that's only part of the story.

At key points throughout the book, you are given the chance to solve puzzles, break codes, work through mazes, answer riddles and even decide the direction of the story.

 Whenever this symbol appears in the text, it means you have a problem to solve or a decision to make before you can go on.

It's not really necessary to solve all the puzzles to enjoy the adventure of the Gold Jaguar but you might feel like you're missing out on something if you don't try . . . like sitting in the movies with your eyes closed.

If you get stuck on a problem, just keep reading. The continuing story will probably offer a hint. And if you're really stumped, try the answer section at the back of the book.

Good luck and watch your step . . . the fate of the Gold Jaguar expedition rests on your ingenuity.

Contents

Metropolitan Telephone Company

Main Office 100 Main Street Mainland, USA 11345

9/9

Dear Resident,

Special attention has been given in our attempts at meeting your demands for improved telephone service. Not all of our customers happen to live in areas of the high density you do, but in our crowded society we do what we can.

You have already called us regarding the breakdown and we repeat...the next few days will not show much improvement. A week must pass before the service will be normal.

Big clients do not get much better service and money does not buy our attention, as you suggested.

Bring this to our notice if it recurs. Our weapon in the fight against competitors is your support.

Prepare for a few day's inconvenience. We will try to have your phone back in working order soon. Take comfort in the knowledge that your phone company's journey to improved communications is proceeding full speed.

All best,

President And Chief Officer

·The more you talk...the richer we get!·

1
Big Mac

The letter from the telephone company was delivered by messenger just after the morning mail arrived. You put it on the kitchen table along with all the other mail: the latest issue of *Fuddles, Muddles and Mazes,* the electric bill, a notice from your library that a book is overdue and a letter from your Aunt Edna about her gall bladder operation. The usual stuff. You read the phone company letter casually over a bowl of oatmeal and are just about to file it in the basket under the sink when something stops you.

Why have they delivered this particular message by messenger? Why is the letter so dull and pointless? What is the Metropolitan Telephone Company anyway? And, you conclude as long as you're in a questioning mood, why aren't messages delivered by messangers?

Then you realize the problem. There hasn't been a breakdown in your phone service! Your phone is phine, you quip. What's going on here, you wonder? Is this just a simple corporate snafu? No, wait a minute, you say...that date! Nines with no year? It's a coded letter from The Society! It's been months since their last communication; you'd almost forgotten about them. The real message is hidden in the letter, and the number nine is the key. But can you remember how to break the code?

Taking out your pencil, you carefully circle the first word beginning with the first sentence and then circle every ninth word throughout the letter. "Aha," you say when you've decoded the whole text, "so there's an adventure afoot." You'll have to put everything else aside and give The Society a hand.

You immediately start to pack your knapsack but stop abruptly. A journey, the note said, but a journey to where? What should you take? The last time The Society contacted you, they had you trudging across the Swiss Alps looking for a hidden uranium lab. That time, you had packed only a sweatshirt and a tennis racket. Then there was the expedition in Haiti when you brought along a down jacket and ski gloves. You wish just once they'd explain where you were going before you got there. But that wasn't the way The Society handled things. No. Everything had to be confidential, top secret, hush-hush.

You do your best, taking both a warm sweater and a bottle of suntan lotion, a change of socks, toothpaste, hiking shoes, and your trusty pad and pencil.

But the weapon? Which one do they want you to take? The ballpoint blowpen? The poison-tipped paper airplane? The matchbox rockets? Or the gun in the shape of a box of Cracker Jack? Going strictly according to whim, you decide on the gun, take it out of the drawer, assemble it carefully and pack it in your sack.

When everything is ready, you sit down for a moment to review the familiar procedure: First it's off to the airport where your tickets will be waiting; you'll land in New Hampshire, where a taxi will take you to a remote little town, then you'll be dropped off at a motel, you'll say the passwords, the door will open and Big Mac will be waiting to explain your next reckless assignment.

A strange hobby you've picked, you mumble as you leave the

house, but there's nobody but yourself to blame. Perhaps it was too many *Mission: Impossible* episodes on television, too many James Bond films or one too many dull mornings eating oatmeal and reading the electric bill. But after all, *you* wanted a little adventure...

The plane ride up to New Hampshire is uneventful. You sleep, dream of turvy-topsy mazes, wake up and eat a snack of potato chips and cheese wedges. When the plane lands, you're the only passenger getting off at this stop. You watch the aircraft refuel and take off again. You are alone in the terminal. Eventually a taxicab pulls up to the door. The solemn-faced driver steps out and walks in your direction. He offers to give you a lift. There's no one else anywhere to be seen. A match made in heaven, you decide, and accept his offer.

Half an hour later you pull up in front of a motel. It's the same old place. The neon NO VACANCY sign is still short circuited, the front door is still missing a hinge and, as always, there don't seem to be any patrons at all. You absentmindedly reach for your money but the cabbie shakes his head. "That's okay," he says, "I've already been paid."

You step out of the car into the cold New England afternoon. Snow is about to burst through the haze. You pull up the collar

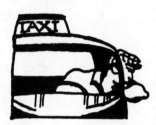

of your down vest, wink back at the NO VACANCY sign that is blinking at you from the front window and head into the office.

In the room, a white-haired lady is sitting at a desk behind the counter, knitting and watching TV. From your angle you can just barely make out a "Man From U.N.C.L.E." rerun on the screen. You lean on the counter and smile. She smiles back, puts down her knitting and with great effort gets up from the chair and saunters over to you. With her flabby elbows resting on the formica top, she adjusts her glasses and speaks.

"Why, hello. Are you looking for a room? I'm afraid we don't have any available today," she says, sounding like every grandmother that ever knitted a pair of booties.

"I see," you say, still trying to shake off the chill, "you're already too full. That's the trouble with our SOCIETY."

"Oh! Oh my," she replies suddenly stiffening, "in that case I suppose I do have a room."

Having gotten those formalities over with, you begin the sequence of codes that you have repeated countless times to grandmothers at this same counter.

"Before you show me the room, would it be possible to order some food?" you begin.

"Yes," she says fixing a strand of hair, "I can order it for you. What would you like?"

"Big Mac."

"I see. With or without?"

"With," you answer. Then, consulting the calendar on the wall and noting it is Thursday, you continue, "And hold the pickles."

You watch her eyes survey the calendar and a puzzled look comes over her face. New wrinkles appear at the corners of her mouth.

"Wouldn't you rather hold the onions?" she asks.

You look at the calendar again. You distinctly recall that yesterday was Wednesday, so you stick with your choice.

"No. Pickles," you insist.

"You don't want to hold the onions?" she asks again, this time pointing to Wednesday with a crooked finger. You also see that her other hand has slowly opened a drawer near her hip and is reaching inside. You grasp the hand resting on the calendar and move her finger over to Thursday.

"Pickles," you say sternly.

"Oh dear," she says catching her mistake and retrieving both hands. "I must be a bit confused. Is it Thursday already? Oh my, why I believe it is. Thursday, yes it really is Thursday. Hold the pickles, of course, you must hold the pickles, dear. Please go right to Room 409 and knock twice. Oh my."

You leave her knitting and mumbling, and walk down to Room 409 at the end of the line of rooms. It is starting to snow lightly. You knock twice on the door. A beefy man in a blue blazer opens it and motions for you to enter. The room is completely dark except for a single spotlight focused in the center of the floor. The guard presses a tiny earpiece deeper into his ear, then directs you to the middle of the floor. You stand in the light, wincing from the glare, and can almost feel the eye of the closed circuit camera giving you an electronic once-over. After a few seconds, a door to your right unlocks and you walk into the next room.

This second room is also dark except for the greenish light of a computer terminal and the slits of gray daylight slicing through the venetian blinds on the window. In front of these blinds sits the shadowy figure of Big Mac. You realize then that you have never actually seen him clearly and as your eyes adjust, you begin to notice that there are two additional people in the room.

"Good, you're here at last. What took you so long?" asks the familiar tenor voice.

"Um…a slight problem with my lunch order," you say.

"Yes, I understand. She almost shot someone last week for wanting a fish sandwich on Monday. I think I have to get myself a new grandmother. Well, anyway, let's begin the meeting."

Following Mac's gesture, the two others step forward into the light. One is a tall man with a thick black beard and the other is a short chubby fellow who seems to be sweating in spite of the frost. Mac begins the introductions.

"I've picked the three of you, and another team member who'll be joining you later, very carefully for this assignment. Your destination is Central America. This is Dr. Paul Dentons," he says pointing to the taller one. "He's an expert on the art, architecture and customs of the Indian tribes in the area. Pancho here," he says indicating the round one, "speaks a number of languages including six or seven of the local Indian dialects in the section of Central America you'll be visiting. All of these skills will come in handy. But if we need anyone on this strange expedition, we're going to need a heuristist like yourself," Mac says pointing in your direction.

"A what?" Pancho asks, showing a weakness in one of his languages.

"A heuristist," Mac repeats.

"What's that?" Pancho asks, speaking for you as well.

"Heuristics, Pancho, is the study of problem solving. Our friend here is an expert in solving problems, in thinking logically, in creative leaps of the mind. So, I've invented the term 'heuristist' to describe that valuable ability."

Before you can interrupt to deny his high opinion of you, Mac continues, "And believe me, we're going to need a real good thinker on this assignment to solve the puzzles."

"Puzzles?" you ask, suddenly perking up. "What puzzles?"

"The puzzles of the Kryptec Indians."

Mac takes a small tack from the top drawer of his desk, holds it in his right hand like a dart and throws it at the wall. Only the sound of its point puncturing the wood proves that it hasn't vanished into the dark. Mac turns on a high-intensity lamp at the corner of his desk and focuses the beam of light on the wall where the tack has found its target on a map of the Western hemisphere.

"Your destination, my friends, is Tortilla. What do you know about Tortilla, Pancho?"

"Tortilla?" Pancho replies, suddenly caught off guard, "I had one for lunch yesterday with guacamole. Real good."

"Forget lunch, Sanza, I'm talking about the Republic of San Tortilla in Central America!"

"Oh, that Tortilla! Well, let's see ... it's the smallest country in the hemisphere ... mostly jungle ... very undeveloped. It's one of the last true democracies left in Central America, but the government is shaky. There's a bunch of right-wing generals

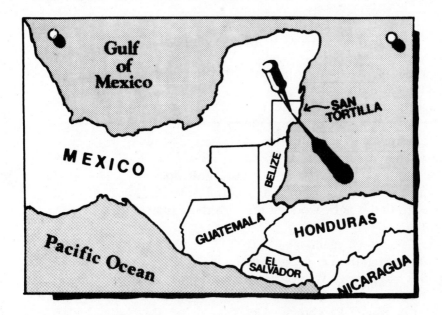

operating out of Belize that are trying to topple the government and take over the place."

"Very good," Mac replies. "That's all quite true. The government there is certainly not on firm ground. They're getting quite desperate for support and funds. For this reason, a member of the Tortillan cabinet has approached The Society with a very intriguing proposition. And, of course, you'll all be paid quite well for your services." Taking the silence as an expression of interest, Mac goes on. "The government of San Tortilla wants us to try to find an object of great financial and cultural significance. It's called the Gold Jaguar."

"*Dios mio! El jaguar de oro!* I knew it!" Pancho blurts.

"You've heard of it then?"

"Oh sure! Everyone down there has. It's part of the folklore, you know, like the tooth fairy. Everybody knows about it, but I don't think anyone really thinks it exists. Does it?"

"That's exactly what we've been hired to find out," Mac replies.

"If my memory serves me correctly," Dr. Dentons breaks in, "the Aztec Indians searched for the Gold Jaguar for years but could never find it. Cortez also hunted for it . . . without any luck."

"That's true, Professor. And it's never turned up on the black market either."

"So how do we know," Dentons continues, "that this jaguar isn't really a wild goose in disguise?"

"We don't. But the government of San Tortilla is very anxious to determine the accuracy of the rumors. Finding it would be a great help in their struggle to stay in power. They feel it would unite the country. They've offered us a substantial reward to locate it, too, but it's not going to be easy. If the jaguar does exist, it's somewhere in the densest jungle in Central America. And the only way to find it is by working through the Kryptec puzzles."

"What puzzles?" you insist again.

"I'll get to that in a minute. Let me give you a little background on this assignment. We don't have much time so I'll have to make it brief."

"Kind of a brief briefing?" Pancho chuckles.

"I'll explain as much as I can now. The rest of the information is in these blue dossiers. You can study them on the plane tonight."

For a moment, Mac's face moves into the streaks of light as he pushes the dossiers across the desk. Deep-set eyes, a prominent nose and a thinning hairline shine momentarily. Then he sits back and begins the explanation.

"Around the eighth century, the Kryptec Indians were a great tribe that lived in the area that is now San Tortilla. The center of their empire was a walled city called Pixtox," Mac says, sounding a 'sh' sound for the x's in the name.

"That's a word in Kryptec," Pancho interjects, "meaning 'neither here nor there.'"

"Exactly. These Kryptecs worshiped the jaguar as the most cunning and clever of their gods. They believed that the jaguar had created the universe as a puzzle world and then placed man in it. All of the art and crafts of the Kryptecs are riddled with … well … riddles and puzzles. The whole purpose of life, according to their mythology, was to be in touch with this puzzle world. Even the city of Pixtox itself was supposed to have been a great maze. At the center of the city was a temple with three doors and inside this temple was a secret burial chamber in which was hidden the crowning achievement of their gold handiwork...the Gold Jaguar."

"If all this were true, why hasn't anyone ever found it?" you ask.

"The Gold Jaguar and the lost city of Pixtox have all faded into myth, history and hearsay. Maybe they're still there, hidden in the jungle somewhere and maybe not. The simple fact is that no one has been interested in San Tortilla for hundreds of years. Most people don't even know it exists. As Pancho said, it's mostly jungle, and unlike the governments of Mexico and Guatemala, the Tortillans haven't been too encouraging to archeologists. There's just no reason to go there. Except in the capital city, the natives still live a very primitive life in the jungle."

Mac placed both hands flat on the desk to give extra support to his next statement.

"Now listen carefully to what I'm about to say. Many of the natives now living in San Tortilla claim to be direct descendants of the ancient Kryptecs. They speak the same language as their ancestors, carry on many of the same customs and still worship the jaguar. They're going to be your best lead but talking to them can be tricky. They tend to speak in riddles," he says pointing a finger at you.

"And so the government wants to find the jaguar, hoping it will gain the support of the Indians, sí?" Pancho asks.

"Exactly. Señor Mentira, the man I met with last week, is the Deputy of Interior Affairs for San Tortilla. He feels that locating the Gold Jaguar will help them rally the Indians and fight off any invasion."

"That's a good idea," Pancho says, "these Indians are pretty superstitious. They'd follow anyone who they thought was on the side of the jaguar. This Mentira is a man of vision."

Mac's face breaks into a rare smirk.

"What's so funny?" Pancho asks.

"Well...it's just that Señor Mentira, this 'man of vision,' had only one eye. He wore an eyepatch over the other. Anyway, are there any other questions?"

"Yes," you blurt out, "about four hundred of them."

"I'm sorry, but I don't have time to answer them. Your plane

CANDY INVESTORS
ASSOCIATION INC.

4 6 ⸾ ⸾ 0 0 0 0 0 1 1 3 0 0 ⸾⸾

Authorized Signature

takes off within the hour and we have other preparations to make. Now, your cover for this assignment is the Candy Investors Association. Here are your IDs. Officially, you are in San Tortilla simply to search for a rare variety of sugar cane known as *Saccharum gigantus,* to be used in gum and candy manufacturing."

You take the plastic card from Mac, sign your name on the front and suddenly realize that you have made the perfect choice in weapons. The Society thinks of everything.

"Only the four of you, Señor Mentira and myself know about the true nature of your mission. Let's keep it that way. This is a top-secret operation. Under no circumstances are you to make contact with agents of the Tortillan government. Obviously, you'll have to avoid any operatives of the right-wing generals. In other words…you're completely on your own until you return. Be careful who you're dealing with, check your sources. The fourth member of your team will meet you in San Tortilla and should be helpful in making the right contacts. Anything else?"

"Yes…"

"Our time is up. Any other information we have is in those blue folders. Study them carefully. Good luck."

Mac stands up stiffly, shakes hands with each of you, then ushers everyone out the front door. From there, you spend a silent and foreboding hour's ride back to the airport, take a quick flight through the growing darkness to Kennedy International Airport, board a routine night flight down to Cancun in Mexico, then make another change to a small, twin-engine plane for the one-hour ride to the only landing strip in Tortilla.

This last leg of the journey is the hardest. The windows creak, the light flickers, and the lumpy seats pummel your spine. The three of you are the only passengers. Feeling safe from prying eyes, Dr. Dentons takes out the dossiers and passes them around. Mac was right about the lack of information. The folders are thin in both data and bulk. As you begin to delve into the smattering of facts, you gaze out the window of the plane at the black clouds billowing against the blacker sky. You wonder exactly why you have elected to risk your life again. For the money? The glory? Because The Society needs you? You wonder if Mac is home in his motel right now, fast asleep, warm and snuggly and dreaming peacefully.

The plane finds a pothole in the air and clatters over it.

2
Tortilla

As the plane bumps and bounces through the equatorial air, you try to read over the dossiers. One of them outlines a survey of the entire country undertaken six years ago by the American Mining Corporation...Aminco. Desperate to find a source of funds, the government of San Tortilla had invited Aminco to send a team of geologists and mining experts to see what they could find. After a year of combing through the jungle, doing plant and soil studies, taking aerial photographs and outlining and plotting the entire landscape, they couldn't find anything worth digging up and exporting. The results were a big zero. Except for several weird beetles, some fat sugar cane plants and a few traces of zinc and tin, the whole country, according to the Aminco team, was just overgrown bush with some scattered Mayan and Kryptec ruins.

You put the report on the empty seat next to you and decide that the only thing of value in all of Tortilla was the fact that nobody ever heard of it. Unless, of course, the Gold Jaguar really existed.

"There's nothing much there," you say aloud.

"You read that Aminco survey?" Pancho asks turning around in his seat. "A year-long search and all they could find was bugs. Nice going."

"So why are these generals so interested in taking over the country?"

"Power, my friend…a much bigger prize than gold. Besides, maybe they like chicle."

"Chicle?"

"Yeah. Chicle. It comes from the sap of the sapota tree. It's Tortilla's only export crop. It's the main ingredient in chewing gum. I worked down there one summer as a *chiclero*. What a lousy job."

"Was it hot?" you ask trying to recall if you packed short pants.

"Not bad. The problem was I had this boss who kept chewing me out…"

A fresh jolt sends Pancho spinning back into his seat.

Another folder explains the history of the region: the rise of the Kryptecs around A.D. 700, the empire they built in the jungle to worship the jaguar god and its puzzle world, the conquest of their nation by the more warlike Aztecs in the twelfth century and then, in 1519, the coming of Cortez and the Spaniards.

"Say, excuse me," Pancho says rubbing his head with one hand and pointing to your open knapsack with the other, "could I have one of those? I love Cracker Jack."

"No, Pancho. Sorry, but these particular ones aren't good for your health."

"Hey, come on, just a few. I won't steal the surprise."

"The surprise in this box is lethal," you say.

"Okay, okay…forget it. *Es tacaño*," he says mumbling into the void.

"It says in this file," you say trying to change the subject, "that Cortez conquered the Aztec empire with only 533 men. That can't be true."

"Oh yeah, it's true. The Aztecs had real lousy luck. See, there was this ancient myth running around the empire about one of their gods…Quetzalcoatl. He had disappeared around A.D. 1000. The myth said he would return in five hundred years from the direction of the rising sun and bring prosperity, you know, like the messiah. Well, in 1519 Montezuma II, the emperor and chief honcho, was anxiously awaiting the return of Quetzalcoatl when who should pop up on the horizon but Cortez, all set to rape and plunder. Naturally, Montezuma thought his god had returned and opened the city up to him. Some welcome mat."

"No worse," Dr. Dentons interrupts, looking up from his own reading, "than the one the Kryptecs offered to their Aztec invaders."

"Yeah, but at least that was Indian business. The Indians at least learned from each other. They shared religions and crafts and stuff. But Cortez? No way. He wanted it all for himself. He just came in and trashed the whole culture."

"Cortez must have been some military genius," you suggest.

"Cortez was a lucky son of a bitch, that's all. As soon as he landed in the New World he met an Indian girl who became his mistress. He called her Doña Marina. As luck would have it, she was a genius at languages. She spoke all the local dialects including Aztec, and she learned Spanish in no time. Without her, Cortez could never have talked the local tribes into rebelling against the Aztecs. That's how he beat two million Aztecs with 533 men. Luck and salesmanship!"

You can see that Pancho is beginning to brood over the whole sad history of ancient Mexico; the Indian part of him sinking to a particularly low point. You try to continue the conversation.

"But also Cortez came from a much more advanced civilization, didn't he? I mean the tribes here..."

"The tribes here," Dr. Dentons says with a professorial frown, "represent some of the highest points in all of western civilization."

"Careful, amigo," Pancho whispers, placing one chubby hand on your shoulder, "I think lecture #1, 'The Civilizations of Mesoamerica,' is beginning."

Before you can change the subject, the lecture is already in progress.

"In talking about the cultures of Mexico and South and Central America, we encounter some of the most civilized societies on earth. From 2000 B.C. all the way up to the sixteenth century, great cities and empires came and went...from Mexico down to Peru and Chile. This means agricultural villages with advanced methods in pottery, crop planning, clothing manufacture, housing and, of course, the great massive metropolitan centers as well. Take, for example, the capital of the Aztec empire...Tenochtitlan. By the time Cortez arrived it was five times the size of London!"

"Holy cow," you say.

"Holy cow indeed. The Maya, Incas, Chichimecs, Toltecs, Nazcas, Aztecs, Olmecs, and our friends the Kryptecs...were all highly complex societies struggling for survival in a hostile environment."

"And don't forget the Hamanecs," Pancho adds as a sudden turbulence sends bags crashing to the floor.

"The Hamanecs?" Dentons asks pulling on his beard, "I've never heard of the Hamanecs. Did they inhabit this region?"

"Hey sure, man, the Hamanecs. You never heard of them? Yeah, they raised chickens and pigs. Every morning they'd take eggs from the chickens and fry up one of the pigs and make themselves a nice breakfast...that's why they're called Hamanecs."

You force out a laugh but Dentons can only manage a sad shake of his head. The door to the cockpit opens and the pilot tells everyone to prepare for landing. You strap your seat belt and grip the armrests as the plane begins its rollercoastering descent.

Outside the small windows, night commands the horizon.

Streaks of moonlight slide through the clouds and bounce off the wings. Visions of jaguar gods, cities of stone and mud and the teeming jungle rise up from below as you plummet toward the ground.

"Who's meeting us?" Pancho shouts, trying to be heard above the roar of his own panic.

"I don't know," Dentons answers. "As usual, Mac didn't explain anything. It's a pilot named Ace Kennedy. Just what I need...more air travel."

"Ace Kennedy? I know Ace. Very interesting person. A well known bush pilot. Real adventurer, too. Some folks think Ace is a smuggler." Another jolt. "Hey, Doc, isn't air supposed to be *soft?*"

The plane finally makes a jittery landing on a small airstrip near the Tortillan border. For the final part of your trip, you throw your bags onto an old minibus and try to settle into the ragged leather seats. To avoid the capital city, you have been scheduled to meet Ace Kennedy at a place called Hojos. The ride there, on the only highway in Tortilla, is enlightening. On either side of the bus, by the eerie light of the moon, the thick jungle seems to stretch to the outer reaches of darkness. Great leaves and grotesque vines bar the way, daring anyone to leave the paved road. The edges of this thin strip of civilization are losing a war with nature, a war the bush has been winning for thousands of years.

"It's going to be this kind of traveling from now on, I'm afraid," Pancho says jiggling at every bump. "Mac said we have to avoid Joe Chemilko at all costs."

"Who's Joe Chemilko? One of the generals?"

"Not who...what. Joe Chemilko is the capital city of San Tortilla."

"That's a bizarre name for a Central American city, isn't it?" you say, reeling from the roadwork.

"It's not that strange," Pancho says with a jounce. "See, when Cortez passed through Tortilla on his way to conquer the Aztecs, he left some men here to keep an outpost. The man in charge of it was his only Prussian officer, a shipbuilder named Joseph Chemilko. Well, it just so happens that the name Joe Chemilko sounds exactly like the word Xochimilco in Nahuatl, the language of the Aztecs. It means 'field of flowers.' So naturally, even after the Spaniards left, the Indians kept the name."

"Weird coincidence."

"Not according to the Kryptecs. They don't believe in coincidence. Or chance. To them everything that happens is planned by the jaguar god," Pancho explains while jolting into the air.

Eventually the bus veers off onto a side road covered with dirt and pulls up to a small bunch of huts with thatched roofs and kerosene lamps burning in the doorways. Small birds seem to be hovering around the lamps.

"This is *it*?," you ask in a stupor, "are we here?"

"Yup, this is it," Pancho answers. "Ace will meet us here in the morning."

"Great. Where exactly are we?"

"Hojos."

"I know, but I mean...what *is* it?"

"This place? It's a village...actually a trading post. We can stay overnight here and get something to eat. That's why they call it Ho Jo's."

You get out of the bus, stand in the middle of nowhere and look around. Three or four Indians are huddling near an open fire. A goat stops munching to look at you, then goes back to its dinner. The charming little birds that seemed so attracted to the lamplight turn out to be enormous insects. A dank chill slips under your skin. Silence crowds the huts from all sides, except for the incessant buzzing of gruesome creatures from the humid leaves.

"Luxurious it ain't," Pancho says breaking the spell, "but who cares. I'm starving. Come on."

Having no other reservations, you follow him into the unknown.

In the morning you are awakened by a small turkey who has decided to nibble on your knapsack. You look around, a bit disoriented at first. Slowly you remember where you are and only then do the turkey, goat, the smell of burning bark and the sounds of strange voices begin to make sense.

Outside your hut, Dr. Dentons and Pancho are eating breakfast with a tall, thin, very attractive woman who is wearing a canvas jacket and a broad-brimmed hat. You join the group and are introduced to Ace Kennedy, the legendary pilot, who soon excuses herself and disappears into one of the huts.

"So that's Ace Kennedy," you say trying to sound awake.

"Yup, that's her. Hey, you look terrible. Here, have some Balche," Pancho says offering you a dark liquid in a wooden cup. "It's real good. Fermented honey and tree bark. It'll wake you up."

The drink tastes like the business end of a donkey but you politely quaff a cup.

"How'd you sleep?" Pancho continues.

"Not as little as I expected."

"Well, I slept wonderfully," Dr. Dentons says. "Better than I've slept in months. These huts are actually quite cleverly designed. The walls are just bunches of sticks lashed together but they allow air to circulate nicely and the layers of leaves on the roofs insulate against the direct sunlight during the day. Real solar planning. The hammocks give you a nice rock while you're sleeping and keep the turkeys out of your hair…"

"Not out of my hair," Pancho says. "All night I dreamed the little buggers were taking revenge for years of Thanksgivings. They were dressing me with cranberry sauce."

Ace Kennedy returns with a small package wrapped in brown paper tucked under her arm. The three of you follow her over to a leafy canopy near the edge of the clearing. You sit down on the ground and watch as Dr. Dentons unwraps the package. Inside the wrapping is a small piece of thick paper on which a series of strange symbols has been painted in black. Dr. Dentons examines it from a few angles, then shrugs and places it on the ground before him.

"This is it? This is the big deal?" he asks Ace.

"That's it."

"How much did you pay for it?"

"Five hundred smackers."

"Doesn't look like it's worth that at all."

"Say, excuse me," Pancho interrupts, "but what exactly is *it*?"

"I had heard this rumor," Ace explains, "about a poem written in code that had been found near one of the Kryptec villages around here. It was supposed to be a translation of an ancient text that led to the lost city of Pixtox and the Gold Jaguar. I didn't think much about it; there are a lot of rumors in Tortilla. But when Mac contacted me about this expedition, I thought I should get hold of it. Maybe it's a good place to start."

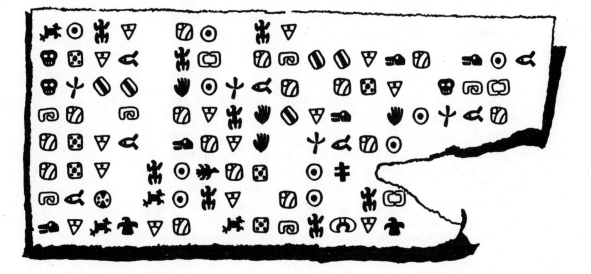

"Sounds good," Pancho says. "Now that we've got it, what do we do with it?"

"Decode it, I guess. What else can we do?" Dentons asks as he picks up the piece of paper from the ground and hands it to you, adding, "Good luck!"

"Good luck? What do you expect me to do with it?" you ask.

"Well, you're the puzzle expert on the team," he replies, "and so far, this is the only clue we have to finding the lost city. Basically, we're stumped until you figure out what it means. Those inscriptions are Kryptec symbols...like hieroglyphs."

"Well, has anyone ever deciphered ancient Kryptec symbols?"

"No. But that's not the problem. Remember, Ace said this is a modern translation of an ancient Kryptec poem. From the look of this paper," Dentons says examining the watermark carefully, "I'd say this was written in the last few years. Someone's taken the trouble to write down that poem in a code so no one else can understand it. Until now?" he adds giving you the scrap again.

"So if it was written down recently," Pancho adds, "even though it uses these old hieroglyphs, the poem could be in any language, right? Spanish or Nahuatl or Dutch or a thousand other languages."

"True," Dentons concurs.

"But luckily for you," Pancho adds, "it's probably in English."

"English??"

"Sure, amigo. It makes sense. English is now the official language of Tortilla. *Habla español?*"

"No."

"Tlix Nahuatl?"

"No."

"Then you'd better start with English," he concludes and slumps down near a tree for a morning siesta.

You stare at the characters for a long time and at first they simply stare back at you blankly. But after a while you notice a familiar pattern, the same kind of pattern you'd expect to find in a normal English paragraph: both long and short words, each word composed of a handful of symbols and only about twenty different symbols in all.

Could it be that simple, you wonder. Could the note be a simple cryptogram with one symbol substituted for each letter in the sentence? Working under that assumption, you get to work trying to crack the code.

Luckily, your first guess turns out to be the clue that breaks the code. It is a cryptogram in English and the single letter does indeed stand for the letter 'a.' Thus, by substitution and elimination, you slowly switch letters of the alphabet for each of the symbols. In a few minutes, you have the puzzle solved and quickly show it to the others, reveling in the new respect you have earned.

"Terrific," Ace says with more than a hint of sarcasm. "Now that we know what it means . . . what does it mean?"

"Beats me," Dr. Dentons answers, "it's a poem all right. And it looks like there's a word missing on the sixth line where the paper is torn. But I don't see how it's a clue to the lost city. Pancho?"

"Sorry, Doc. I don't get it either."

"We'll have to show it to a member of the Kryptec tribe," Dentons continues, "and see what they have to say about it. Are any of the people in this village Kryptecs?" Dr. Dentons asks Ace.

"No. The Kryptecs live in villages farther up north. Is that where you want to start?"

"Yes, I think that's the best place to begin," Dentons responds. "Ace, are you on good terms with any of the village elders or any of the Kryptec chiefs?"

"The Kryptecs don't have tribal chiefs. There are some old Indians around who we can try to talk to . . . who know a lot of tribal history and lore. The problem is, the older they are the more they tend to talk in riddles. But we can try."

"Yeah," Pancho adds, "the Kryptecs have one word, *tlox,* that means both to finish solving a puzzle and to grow older."

"Well, this sounds like our best bet, let's get going," Dentons says and you leave to get your belongings.

Gathering again in the clearing, you follow Ace as she picks her way through the leaves down a narrow path through the jungle. Half a mile away there is another clearing that has been hacked out of the wilderness. It is a long rectangular strip where the grass has been stomped down flat. At the far end is a small single-engine airplane. You march toward it quietly as the sun begins to heat up the terrain.

"What's this?" Dr. Dentons says with a hint of terror in his voice.

"What's what?" Ace asks as she pulls on a pair of beaten leather gloves.

"We're not going up in this contraption, are we?" he says pointing a shaking finger.

"Contraption? I've logged over 4,000 hours in Bimbo here. She's the best little buggy this side of the Rio Grande. She'll get us there all right."

"Bimbo?" you repeat to Pancho who returns your shrug.

"You mean this thing actually flies?" Dentons continues in a whine.

"Are you kidding? This is a vintage 1925 Curtiss biplane. It's a classic. What's the problem?"

"1925? Hadn't they invented aerodynamics by then?"

"Look, Professor," Ace answers practically spitting out the middle syllable, "do you want a lift to the Kryptec villages or not? If not, save me an afternoon and start hiking." She points through the jungle in the general direction of oblivion.

"Perhaps we should carry Bimbo just to be safe..."

"Come on," you say as you help Pancho hoist Dentons into the plane, "we'd better get going. What's the worst thing that could happen? We could conk out over the jungle, crash dive into a swamp and get eaten by cannibals, that's all. It could be worse."

"There's no cannibals in Central America," Pancho corrects.

"There, see what I mean? It could always be worse," you say and with a gulp...hop into Bimbo yourself.

Once inside, it is clear that Dentons is still in a panic. Partly to calm him down, Ace talks him through the takeoff procedure. Since you are sitting in the copilot's seat, you are forced to follow the routine as well.

"Look, Professor," Ace begins, "flying is really very simple. There's nothing to it. First I put the key in the ignition and turn her on...just like a car. Then I pull the throttle one quarter of the way and watch this gauge go up to ten. When it hits ten... we start to move."

Following the spinning propeller, Bimbo begins to shudder and roll down the grassy runway.

"Now we simply increase the speed by pulling the throttle out slowly, take off the brake by turning it to the left and pushing it in and when the gauge hits eighty...we're off."

You watch Ace follow her own instructions, take tight hold of the wheel and just as you hit eighty knots on the dial...you're airborne and the ground drops away below.

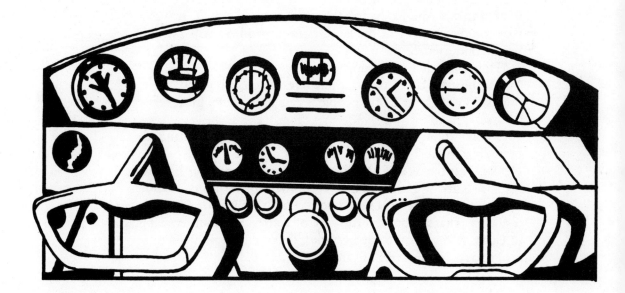

"Now that wasn't too bad, was it? It's only five steps... ignition, throttle, brake, throttle and steer. And steering is fun; push the wheel in and we go down, pull it back and we go up, turn and we turn. See?"

Ace takes the aircraft through a series of swoops and swerves to illustrate her points. With each loop, Dentons seems to turn a darker shade of green. But you actually begin to develop a warm and friendly feeling toward Bimbo. Now that you're in the air, the clattering buzz you took to be loose joints has taken on a pleasant murmur. Ignition, throttle, brake, throttle, steer. Not too difficult at all.

At one point during the flight, Ace turns around to read a map and leaves the wheel in your hands. Overcoming your fear, you take the controls and in a few moments are happily flying by yourself high above the jungles of San Tortilla. You make a mental note to look into ground school when you get back home.

"If the lost city of Pixtox really exists," you say looking out the window and shouting above the wind, "shouldn't we be able to see it from the air?"

"Not really," Ace says taking command again, "Tortilla is small but it's not that small. There's still plenty of area to cover, even from the sky. Besides, after that Aminco survey a few years ago, everybody lost interest in trying to find the lost city. They figured that if Aminco hadn't found it, nobody would. It was a very complete survey of the land. I was down here while it was being conducted."

"How big was Pixtox supposed to be anyway?"

"I've heard it covered about ten acres. It probably had a population of about 2,000 people," Pancho screams from the back seat.

"I don't know," you say scanning the landscape, "that sounds pretty big to me."

"No. Not big at all," Dentons says removing a paper bag from his lips. "City of Chan Chan in Peru, the capital of the Chimor empire, was twenty times the size of Pixtox. It had 65,000 residents. That's about the capacity of Yankee Stadium. And Tikal in Guatemala was on 6 square miles, that's almost 4,000 acres! So Pixtox...really...isn't...that big...HUP!"

Dentons' last words are lost into the brown bag as Ace veers off in the direction of the sun.

"There's the strip," she shouts pointing to a thin brown line etched into the deep green growth below. "Hang on, this can get a little bumpy."

"God, no!" Dentons groans.

The wings of the plane seesaw over the treetops as she glides Bimbo to the runway. True to her word, you bounce off the dirt, come down and bounce again but with less gusto. The third rebound bumps you off your seat and sends Dr. Dentons deep into the paper bag. Soon the old rattletrap comes to a jittery, grinding stop.

Ace turns off the engine, applies the brake, gets up and shoves open the door. "All out," she says with a heave-ho.

"Just about," Dentons says with a heave.

3

Kryptecs

You spend the day in another village very similar to the one called Hojos, with its thatched huts, hammocks, goats and turkeys and open fires. But as you wander around you begin to notice one difference. These natives seem more distant and mysterious, as if they had secrets that reached back into their own glorious and tragic past.

For much of the afternoon you, Pancho and Dr. Dentons stroll around the village while waiting for Ace to confer with the village elder. Coming upon a trio of Indians who are eating around a fire, you are surprised by the way one of them offers you cornbread.

"Hey, want a bite of some cornbread? Good stuff," he says.

You decline, but turning to Pancho you say, "He speaks English?"

"Sure," Pancho answers. "Like I told you, English is the official language. A lot of the Indians speak it. But Tortilla is completely multilingual. See, in the heyday of the Kryptec civilization, everyone spoke Kryptec. Some of them still do, especially when dealing with tribal matters. When the Aztecs conquered them, everybody had to learn to speak the Aztec language, which is called Nahuatl. And a lot of folks still use that. Then when Cortez came, everybody had to learn Spanish and that was the official language of Tortilla until the arrival of

the American Marines in the 1920s when suddenly all of Tortilla was talking like John Wayne. It's a real language stew... not to mention all the local Indian dialects. *Donde* can I find the *lopocoatatl?*' That's how you ask for the john in modern Tortilla," Pancho says with a beaming grin.

"Did you find out anything?" Dr. Dentons asks Ace, who has now rejoined the group.

"He said he would offer us a pound of $10 gold pieces or a half pound of $20 gold pieces—whichever is worth more—to go home and forget about Pixtox and the jaguar."

"That's great," Dentons replies, "we're already being bribed. I wonder what he's hiding."

"Excuse me, Doc, but I don't think this village elder wants us to take the bribe. He just wants us to answer the riddle," Pancho suggests.

"What riddle?"

"Which is worth more... a pound of $10 gold pieces or a half pound of $20 gold pieces?"

"Why do you say that?"

"Because I know the way the Kryptecs think. This is the way they deal with tribal matters. They won't offer any information until you show your respect to the jaguar god by solving one of their puzzles."

"All right," Ace says, "it's worth a try. I'll go back and tell him we'll take the pound of $10 gold pieces and see what he says."

"Yeah," Pancho agrees, "good idea. But you'd better give him the right answer— which is the half pound of $20 gold pieces!"

Predictably enough, an argument ensues among Ace and Pancho and Dr. Dentons, who thinks that they're both worth the same. As the only arbiter—and the resident brain—it's up to you to provide the correct answer.

It takes only a few moments for you to see the one relevant piece of information—the weight of the gold—and give Ace the right answer. She disappears into the hut again and the three of you continue to mull around the Indians near the fire. When she emerges, she has a bit more information about Pixtox and the poem.

"Well, he says the lost city really does exist. What's left of it is still out there in the jungle. He was taken there as a little boy. But he can't remember exactly where it is because he hasn't left this village in over sixty years. He remembers that there was a separate temple that pointed the way to the lost city."

"That must be what this part of the poem means '...will point the way at a temple's point,'" Pancho suggests reading from your translation.

"I guess so. Anyway, he doesn't know where this temple is either but he thinks there *are* Indians in Tortilla who know more about the location of the lost city. He told us to contact his brother's cousin in a village not too far from here."

"Did you show him the poem?"

"Yes, I showed him the original and our translation. He didn't know anything about it."

"What'd he say about the torn part?"

"He said it looked like there was a piece missing."

"Great. What about the Gold Jaguar, did he know anything about that?"

"He said he remembered seeing it when he was a boy. He was taken through the city to a tall building with three doors called the Temple of the Jaguar..."

"Just like the legend," Pancho says, "now we're getting somewhere."

"Inside there was a secret chamber where the Gold Jaguar itself was kept. He said it was solid gold, too heavy for two men to lift, with teeth made of diamonds and emerald eyes."

"Holy smokes!"

"And ruby claws."

"Nonsense," Dentons huffs, "I don't believe it. How could a treasure like that be kept hidden for all these years? It's impossible."

"Well, I'll tell you one thing, Doc," Pancho insists, "if anyone could do it, the Kryptecs could."

"That's what the old man said," Ace continues, "but who knows if any of it is true? In any case, it's our only lead. We'd better try to find his brother's cousin. We can bunk down here for the night and get an early start in the morning."

Later that night you are lying in your sleeping bag. Unable to sleep, you try to strike up a conversation with Pancho.

"Do you really think the Kryptecs could have kept the Gold Jaguar hidden for all these centuries?" you ask.

"Maybe. See, most of the people in Tortilla are Mestizo—part Spanish and part Indian, after centuries of you-know-what with the conquistadores. But these tribes out here in the bush are pure Kryptec. They don't trust outsiders. They don't trust anyone who doesn't believe in the puzzle world. This Gold Jaguar is sacred to them. I can see them guarding it very carefully. And I don't blame them either. Their ancestors didn't use gold for money; they made beautiful things from it because they believed gold was a gift from the jaguar god. The Spanish destroyed everything when they came over here; they took the gold, melted it down and bought cannons for the navy. That's bad."

Dr. Dentons, who is also having trouble sleeping, pipes up from the far side of the fire. "Unfortunately for the Indians, this whole area was rich in gold. It was ripe to be exploited by the Spanish. They took 25,555 pounds of gold from Mexico and Peru. Let's see…that's…" (Dentons does some quick calculations in his head) "…almost 200 million dollars in modern currency."

"Is there still gold here to be exploited?" you ask, beginning to get drowsy.

"Well, according to the Aminco survey, there isn't. Not in Tortilla anyway. Unless, of course, there are some artifacts still buried in the ruins."

"There's nothing of any value left in the ruins, Doc. Believe me, the *huaqueros* have taken everything of value."

"The who?" you ask, half snoring your question.

"*Huaqueros*...the grave robbers. *Huacas* are burial sites. The *huaqueros* dig them up to find gold and artifacts to sell on the black market."

"Or the gray market."

"Gray market?" you mutter.

"Yes. A lot of museums and organizations buy from suspicious sources to get a good piece for their collections."

"So between the huaqueros, museums, universities, private collectors and the black market the gold is *Pffft!*"

"At least the artifacts get saved," you say, dreaming the last few words of the sentence.

"Well, only if they're worth more than their weight in gold. Otherwise they're melted down and sold as bullion. Do you know the biggest use of gold in the United States?"

"Teeth?" you say from the depths of dreamland.

"Class rings," Pancho answers. "No kidding. Fifteen tons of gold are used every year to make class rings. How do you think the ancient Kryptecs would feel about that? All their fine sacred gold artwork melted down so some pimply kid can prove he finished high school. Does that make sense?"

No answer from you. Dentons has the final word.

"Well, there's always the chance that even the greediest of the *huaqueros* never figured their way through the Kryptec puzzles to the jaguar's chamber."

In the morning, after dreams of gold, the sunlight awakens you. Pancho, already up and busy, offers you some strong coffee and *zaca*, a patty of cornmeal and water.

"This is great, Pancho," you say, "it tastes like glue."

"Hey, *zaca* is an old Indian recipe. I thought it would help you get into the spirit of Tortilla. Every culture has its grain and water delicacy...gruel, pita, oatmeal, rye bread. You have to eat like an Indian to think like one."

"I think I'd rather not think."

"That reminds me, I had this dream last night I was in Chichén Itzá, the ancient city in Mexico. I had opened up a fast food stand there called Chicken Bitza. What d'ya think?"

"Har, har," you respond. "Just pass me the solvent, my tongue is glued in place."

Once the usual morning banter is over, Ace and Dr. Dentons leave to get directions to the next village. Meanwhile you and Pancho break camp and take some time out to stroll around the grounds. Behind one of the huts you come upon a woman weaving a rug. She is using a hip loom, which Pancho informs you is the traditional method of weaving. A strap around her hips keeps tension on the loom as she guides the shuttle back and forth.

"*Zipzipzip*," Pancho says pointing to the incomplete fabric.

"*Tlu. Zipzipzip*," she answers without looking up.

Turning back to you Pancho says proudly, "She speaks Kryptec."

"*Zipzipzip* sounds like Yankee to me," you say trying not to play the fool.

"No, it's really Kryptec. The word *zip* means to go in one direction. *Zipzipzip* means to go back and forth, like the shuttle on her loom . . . in other words, to weave."

"Come on, Pancho," you say, refusing to be made fun of.

"Really," he insists. "Indian languages are very musical. For example, there's a suffix in Hopi—*ta*—that means a series of little actions. *Ripi* means 'it gives a flash' but *ripipita* means 'it is sparkling' . . . lots of little flashes. Nice, huh? In Kryptec the ending *noc* is used the same way. *Cal* means to have a strange thought. *Calnoc* means to have a lot of strange thoughts but *calnocnocnoc* means to be stark raving mad."

Not knowing whether or not to believe him, you turn your attention to the fabrics hanging on a nearby pole.

"These are nice, Pancho. They all have that crooked homemade look," you say following the wavy horizontal lines with your finger.

"My friend," Pancho says, "the Kryptecs are much better weavers than they seem at first glance."

You look carefully at the rug hanging before you and assume from Pancho's remark that it contains some Kryptec trick. But what exactly is it, you wonder.

Holding the edge of your writing pad up to the fabric, you realize the truth of his statement. The fabric design was a lot harder to weave than you first thought.

When Ace and Dr. Dentons return, you are off again on a hike through the jungle to another village. Following the narrow path, you begin to understand why the view from the airplane was deceiving. The thick jungle growths create a dense canopy over the tiny villages and connecting paths that dot the landscape. The throbbing life of the jungle is hidden from the sky. You walk single file behind Ace who swings her machete at invading leaves as mauve monkeys, scarlet and orange parrots, blue hummingbirds and black-billed toucans chatter and dart through the greens.

In a half hour, as the sun begins to bake everything below, including the top of your head, you arrive at the village. The man you are to contact is sitting in front of his hut smoking a cigar. He is a young man and wears only a vest, shorts and a hat. As soon as he hears that you have been sent by his cousin's brother regarding the lost city, he refuses to speak anything but Kryptec. Pancho steps forward and conducts a very brief conversation in the clipped tones of the language.

"He says he can help us find the lost city, but first we have to solve the pebble problem," Pancho explains.

"O Jesus, come on," Ace says in sweaty desperation. "Tell him to show us where it is or his pebbles won't be worth…"

Ace taps the handle of the rifle she has been wearing over her shoulder but Pancho grabs her hand and holds it tightly.

"No, no, Señorita," he implores, "he's a Kryptec. Remember, these puzzles are part of their religion. To defy him would be an insult to the jaguar god. We have to solve the puzzle first."

Ace relents and quite automatically, your three companions step aside to allow you to stand directly in front of the Indian. With weathered hands, he takes out four round pebbles from a burlap pouch and places them on the ground between you, at the four corners of a square. He looks up through the glinting sunlight, winces, passes his hand over the pebbles and says *Tlaloc Chitlit.*

Pancho translates.

"He says here are the four gods of the heavens...maize, water, blood and light. They stand at the four corners of the earth. He asks you to move only two of them, and in so doing to double the size of the earth."

"He said all that?"

"Yeah. Kryptec is a very compact tongue. Anyway, I think he wants you to move two of the stones—and only two—to make a square twice as big as this one here. Can you do it, amigo?"

Visualizing the removal of two stones at a time, you soon hit on the solution by trial and error and make your moves. The Indian sitting on the ground before you seems untouched by your brilliance. Still adamant about speaking only Kryptec, he turns to Pancho and the two of them trade syllables. Pancho turns back to your group.

"He says to find the lost city we must first locate the four guardian temples. They are all near the lost city but only one of them actually points the way. That's the meaning of the first part of the poem."

"What does 'my tallest son' refer to? The tallest of the four guardian temples?"

"He doesn't know."

"Well, where are these temples?"

"He doesn't know that either, but he says that his uncle's sister's daughter knows. She lives in a camp a few miles over thataway," he says pointing west.

"He said all that in those few words?" Dr. Dentons asks suspiciously.

"Yeah. He also said that for the right price he'll give us a note that we can show to her so she'll know to trust us."

"That's fine, but can we trust *him?*" Ace asks in a whisper. "I'm getting a little sick of all these games."

"Look," Pancho answers, "we have no choice. These are the only people who know the location of the lost city."

"If it's anywhere," you add.

"Well, *I've* got a choice," Ace answers. "I say we give up on this whole extended family and start all over again. The *huaqueros* will know where the lost city is, they know the countryside better than anyone. And we won't have to play Alice in Wonderland to find it out from them. We'll just have to pay for the information."

"No, Señorita, I disagree. The *huaqueros* will have us running around in circles. The information we get from these Kryptecs is based on tribal folklore; they have to be honest about it. We can trust what they say."

"Assuming we can guess what they're saying."

"But that's part of their religion. These puzzles have been developed over the centuries to protect the jaguar god. They have to do it this way."

The Indian meanwhile has removed some slips of paper from his pocket. He motions to a small boy to come nearer, mumbles to him in Spanish, then turns to you. Holding the paper at arm's length, he says in rather perfect English…

"This boy will take you to my uncle's sister's daughter. But my friend," he continues in a raspy whisper, "you must be on your guard against the assassins of Mac…"

The words stop abruptly. His eyes roll back, a gasp of air escapes and he keels over onto his stomach. You gaze at each other bewildered. Ace unslings her rifle and runs to the edge of the forest. But there is no one to be seen. On closer examination, you find

a small dart carved from bamboo and fitted with chicken feathers sticking out of the Indian's back.

"I sure hope the price is right," you say solemnly as you remove the paper from his late grip. There are five scraps of thick homemade paper, each with black geometric markings.

"What was he saying just before he…"

"I didn't catch it," Pancho answers.

"That's it. I've had it," Ace grumps in no uncertain terms. "I'm heading back to the village where we left Bimbo. The Indians there will be able to help us locate some of the grave robbers. And they'll know the location of the four guardian temples. Are you coming?"

"This is bad, amigo," Pancho whispers to you. "I think we should follow this lead. The Kryptecs won't trust us if they think we're in cahoots with the *huaqueros*. They obviously want to help us but they have to do it in their own way. I think we should go visit this guy's uncle's sister's daughter with these pieces of paper. What do you think?"

You take a minute to consider the alternatives. You can go with Ace and Dr. Dentons back to the village to start a new line of inquiry, or you can go with Pancho and continue trying to get help from the Kryptecs. Which is the best course of action?

If you decide to go with Ace, turn to page 45.
If you decide to go with Pancho, read on.

You follow the boy along another winding path through the leaves. You imagine snakes, tarantulas and jaguars hiding in the foliage ready to pounce, but the boy seems unafraid and you try to mimic his jaunty gait. He guides you, not to a village, but to a huge chunk of carved stone lying in a clearing.

"What's this?" Pancho asks.

"My cousin said to take you here first. You have to show her the right one, the one that matches," he says pointing to the paper scraps you are holding.

You turn to Pancho for help, but he has already collapsed on a rock and is calmly waiting for you to pick the one piece of paper that matches the pattern on the stone tablet.

 Turn to page 41 and find the one scrap of paper that matches the pattern.

It takes you a few minutes to compare the shapes. You tell the boy that you've made your choice and then it's back through the jungle for a short hike to the next village. Once there, the boy introduces you to the uncle's sister's daughter. You hand her the correct piece of paper. At first, she is quite distraught about the news that her mother's brother's nephew has been killed. She seems confused and unwilling to help. But after a while she regains her composure, thinks for a few moments, then turns to Pancho and speaks... in Kryptec. When she has finished, Pancho turns to you and repeats her statement.

Well, my friend, here's what she says. "If *chla* is not *tlic,* then the answer is *chla,* unless *tlic* is not *tlic,* in which case the answer is *tlic,* unless the answer is *chla.* What is the answer?"

You, of course, are starting to get used to the Kryptec way of doing things. Pancho needs only to repeat the riddle once more for you to get the answer, which he then repeats to the woman. Unimpressed, she simply directs you to walk three hundred paces to the northeast. You and Pancho turn in that direction.

"That's where the lost city is?" you ask in disbelief.

"No, she says it's a way of speaking to the jaguar god who hides inside the lost city. The jaguar will tell us how to proceed. She has seen one of the assassins use it."

"Assassins! That's what the Indian who was killed was saying. Something about assassins. Ask her…"

But by the time you turn your attention back to the woman, she is gone. Only a shadowless chill remains in her place. With no other options, you follow her instructions into the bush. Pancho uses the butt of his rifle to push aside the leaves as you count out the paces.

"Say, Pancho, is every Kryptec in Tortilla related? They sure keep track of their family members."

"They probably are related in one way or another. Most tribal cultures have very complicated family structures. It's important to their social interactions, kind of like knowing who's in what position in a large corporation. It's not unusual...hey look!"

The object of Pancho's interest is a large stone stele—a carved slab—sitting in the jungle. There doesn't seem to be anything too unusual about it. It merely looks like thousands of forgotten carvings that have spent the last few centuries gathering moss. But as you examine the stone, trying to figure out why the woman directed you to it, you notice that there *is* something strange, a familiar pattern which you quickly point out to Pancho.

"Well, one thing is certain," you say, "this sure isn't an authentic ancient carving."

"How do you know that?" he asks.

"Look at it carefully. Look at this group of carvings. What does it look like?"

"Oh! Holy tamale, I see what you mean," he says after you have pointed out the obvious. "What the hell is this for?"

The two of you examine the stele carefully and soon discover a small wire leaving the base of the stele in the back and going into the ground.

"Look at this," Pancho says, "it's a telephone wire. This thing is a damn phone booth."

Try as you might, however, you can't find a receiver anywhere on the slab. You poke the buttons, fiddle with the wire, say "hello" repeatedly into the humid air but you can't seem to make a connection.

"Look, let's get back to the village and see what Dr. Dentons makes of this," Pancho suggests, finally giving in to defeat.

"Swell," you say, giving in to the sweltering heat.

Turn to page 47.

Back at Bimbo, you help Ace load some extra supplies into your backpacks: dried food in foil pouches, flashlights, water purifying tablets, and a box of Cracker Jack that she tosses in your direction.

"Here, I notice that you like this stuff."

"Oh sure. Thanks," you say, caught off guard.

"Don't eat them, though, you'll blow your teeth off."

"Sugar?"

"Bullets. It's an extra magazine of ammo for that ridiculous pistol you're carrying around. Mac really comes up with some winners sometimes. I almost killed myself with the apple grenade last year."

"Well, thanks anyway."

In the village, Ace locates a native trader she has known and asks him about some of the local *huaqueros*. But as luck would have it, he turns out to be a Kryptec. Knowing she cannot understand his language, with great anxiety and hesitation, he resorts to Spanish.

"What does he say?" you ask innocently.

"He says his nephew is sick."

"That's too bad."

"He says he asked his sister to get medicine for the boy but she refused because she doesn't have a nephew. How is that possible?"

You think for a minute, then come up with the answer which seems to satisfy the man and he continues his conversation with Ace.

"What does he say now?"

"He says that an old map showing the four guardian temples was sold a few weeks ago to a group of *huaqueros* camping out up near El Arbol. That's an old Qualia tree farther up along the Oozo."

"The Oozo? What's that?"

"That," she answers pointing behind you. You turn around

and stare into the brush. In the geometric spaces between leaves and stalks you can see the glint of sunlight dancing on water.

"The Oozo runs almost all the way across Tortilla down to the Gulf of Mexico; it's never wider than a few hundred feet," Ace explains. "The Kryptecs of course think it's sacred. It's supposed to be the tears of the jaguar or something. Let me find out if he knows which *huaqueros* bought the map."

The discussion continues in Spanish, leaving you to contemplate the antics of a peccary—a piglike animal—as it noses around in the dirt. Something about its jittery dance reminds you uncomfortably of yourself and so you turn back to Ace, hoping for progress.

"So?" you ask.

"Before he answers my question he wants you to drop this egg three feet without breaking its shell," she says holding out the egg as if it were rotten.

You drop the egg three feet without breaking its shell. You smile. Ace shakes her head.

"Manero," says the Indian sadly.

Turn to page 47.

"Let me get this straight, Pancho," Ace says in disbelief when you've met up again over a pot of coffee, "you found a telephone booth in the middle of the jungle?"

"Yup. It was some kind of intercom or telephone or something. It had pushbuttons. Just couldn't figure out how to use it."

"Did you follow the wire to see where it went?" Dr. Dentons asks.

"Couldn't. It went right into the ground. It was completely buried."

"And what about the woman who told you about it, or the boy who..."

"Couldn't find either of them. They weren't back at the encampment. They disappeared."

"Now what would a phone booth be doing in the middle of the jungle?"

"Beats me. She said she had seen one of the assassins using it to speak to the jaguar god who lives in the lost city. Does that make any sense to you, Doc?"

"No, it doesn't. Perhaps we should try to find this woman again and question her."

"No, we don't have time. I think we should move on. I found out the name of some *huaqueros* who bought a map that's supposed to show the location of the four guardian temples. The leader's called Manero. I know him, a real thief. But we'd better try to find them before they move further into the jungle. Are you coming with us, Pancho, or do you still want to hang around and play games with these Kryptecs?"

"I'm coming... but I still think the Indians are our best bet."

"Then why don't they just tell us where the lost city is?"

"Maybe they don't really know."

"Then they could tell us how to find out."

"But that's exactly what they *are* doing... in their own way. Besides, I think they're scared of something."

"Jaguar voodoo?"

"Maybe. Or maybe someone else doesn't want us to get to Pixtox. Los Generales, for example."

"Who?" you hoot, afraid that there is a new twist in the plot.

"You know, the right-wing generals, the ones who want to

take control of the government. Maybe they've gotten to the Kryptecs before us."

"Well, if the generals know about us," Dentons suggests calmly, "then there's nothing to worry about. We'll just never make it, that's all. We'll join the ruins in immortality."

"Probably right," Ace concurs and then, slipping a long slender bullet into the chamber of her rifle, "…but from now on I'm staying on the alert." And turning to you she continues, "If I were you I'd keep my Cracker Jack cracking."

4
Manero

You wake up the next morning to the sounds of another summit meeting taking place over the embers of the fire. At first the sounds drift in and out, hardly making sense, but as your ears slowly start to function again, you realize that a new decision is in the works.

"No more wild goose chases," Ace says putting her foot down. "How do you know she's telling the truth?"

"Look," Dr. Dentons insists, "she says she knows how to locate the guardian temples. What can we lose by checking it out?"

"Time," Ace replies.

"Our heads," Pancho adds.

"Okay, why don't you two go on ahead and the two of us," Dentons says including you in his broad gesture, "will look into this. We'll catch up with you later by hiring one of the native boys to help us find you."

Then turning to you, Dr. Dentons continues, "I think this is an interesting lead. An old Kryptec woman says she knows a way to find the guardian temples. Are you with me on this little excursion?"

*If you decide to go with Dr.
Dentons, read on.
If you decide to go on ahead
with Ace and Pancho, turn to
page 54.*

"Good luck, amigo," Pancho says patting you on the back,
"we'll see you in a few hours. You know, I just heard from one
of the natives that they don't call the lost city Pixtox any more."

"No?"

"No. They've changed its name to Huerizit, on account of its
strange location."

"Really? Where is it?"

"See what I mean?" he says with a grin and waves goodbye.

Naturally, the old woman that you and Dr. Dentons meet
begins your conversation with a riddle. The boy that Dentons
has hired as a guide translates her question from Kryptec into
Spanish and Dentons repeats it to you in English.

"I hope I've got this right. My Spanish is a little rusty. I think
she asked...is there the same amount of dirt in a hole ten feet
by ten feet by ten feet as there is in a hole five feet by five feet
by twenty feet?"

"That's too easy," you say and give her the answer without any
calculations.

"Oh yes, of course," Dentons says and two translations later
you are back on track.

The woman, quite nonchalant about the speed of your reply,
takes an old photograph out of her pocket and hands it to you.
Then she mumbles something to your guide and you are off
once again.

"You know, Professor," you say as you swat bugs during the
trek, "we seem to be going to an awful lot of trouble for a jaguar
that no one is sure even exists."

"I know," he says catching a frond in the puss, "I'm beginning to wonder about this whole expedition. All this intrigue. Pancho could be right, it could just be an elaborate native religion. But who are these assassins? Who else would be interested in us or in the Gold Jaguar?"

"Maybe there's something else at stake here. Like diamonds or rubies."

"According to the survey, there's nothing like that in Tortilla. And I certainly don't believe that nonsense about the idol having emerald eyes or ruby claws. What about cocaine?"

"What's the most valuable thing in the world, Professor?"

"Information."

"That means the more we find out, the more dangerous it is for us."

"I'll tell you one thing I'd like to find out...how to get out of here in one piece!" he says ducking the attack of an insect the size of a large cheese enchilada.

After a short but sweltering hour, you arrive at your destination, a small temple from which some of the jungle growths have been cleared. It is a tiny stone building, barely large enough for two people to stand up in. Your guide points to the open door, then sits down impassively at the side of the entrance. Cautiously, you follow Dr. Dentons into the structure. A large hole in the ceiling lets bolts of light into the otherwise blank room. It is an empty chamber except for a single carving on the far wall. This is a circular design, intricately carved in bold relief. Dr. Dentons takes out the old photograph given to him by the woman and holds it up in comparison.

"Well, this is it. Okay," he says, "now what?"

"What is it?" you ask.

"It's an ancient Kryptec calendar. Everybody associates it with the Aztecs, but in fact they stole the design from the Kryptecs. To them it was a calendar but also a game..."

"Naturally."

"...the game of life and time. The jaguar god had two sons—

Xol who was the sun and the god of corn, and Macuilzochitl who was the moon and the god of games. That's him in the middle there. When people came here to pray to him they were setting the date for the harvest and also playing the game of time…"

"Wait a minute, Professor. Is that photo for real?"

"I guess so. It looks authentic. Why?"

"Because *that* photograph doesn't show *this* carving, that's why."

"What do you mean?"

"Well, take a look. Look carefully. They're not exactly the same. See the difference?"

*Compare the images
on pages 52 and 54.*

Rather than spending the time examining both images in detail, you hit on a simpler approach. Holding the photograph up before the carving, you position it until the two match in size, as though one followed the other in the pages of a book. When you quickly flip the front image, a difference becomes obvious.

"Good heavens, you're right!" Dentons exclaims and, spurred on by your discovery, he takes out a small magnifying glass and starts to examine the wall in detail. Soon another discovery comes to light.

"This isn't even stone. This is concrete! This wall has been made recently, cast in concrete. Look at the edges up close. They're not chipped at all but smooth, as though they were formed in a mold."

"Why would anyone want to fake a whole wall like this?"

"I can't imagine."

Further inspection reveals that the central stone can be removed. Behind it you find a dial with calibrations around the edge and a needle flicking slightly at the top.

"It's measuring the flow of something," Dentons says.

"Electricity?" you say drawing on your lack of knowledge.

"I don't know," Dentons answers drawing only a blank. "We'd better catch up with Ace and Pancho. This is funny business."

Turn to page 54.

"Well, what'd you find out?" Ace asks Dentons as she finishes setting up her tent.

"Nothing much, just a prefabricated carving and a tiny meter hidden in a phony temple," Dr. Dentons answers.

"Meter? What kind of meter?"

"I really don't know. It looked like the kind that measures flow rates, like some kind of fluid or electricity. But I couldn't say for sure. Did you find out anything about your *huaqueros?*"

"One of the guides said that Manero is somewhere in this vicinity. After we finish setting up camp we can go look for him."

"Are we safe setting up tents like this in the middle of

nowhere?" Dentons asks looking around suspiciously.

"You're never safe in the jungle," Ace answers. "But stay near the fire and don't just roam around by yourself. And watch out for snakes, wild boars, cannibal ants, poisonous plants..."

"Poisonous *darts,*" Pancho adds.

"Right. And don't shoot any jaguars. Remember...they're sacred in this part of the world."

Dentons nervously eyes all the phantoms skulking in the surrounding bush, then quickly finishes pitching his tent and sits at the entrance with his loaded rifle. Pancho gathers together some rocks to make a base for the evening's fire but stops suddenly and stares at the ground.

"Hey! This is weird," he says pointing at his feet.

"Why, is one bigger than the other?" you ask.

"Not my feet, man, *this!*"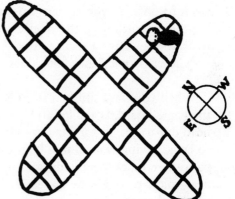

You all gather at the spot where Pancho is standing to discover that a crosslike shape has been etched into the dirt.

"That guide must have put this here before he left. That's a pretty strange thing to do," Pancho says.

"What is it?" you ask.

"It's a patolli board," he explains. "Patolli was a game the Kryptecs and the Aztecs used to play. It's like parchisi. You move stones along the arms of those crosses and try to get your pieces into the middle section."

"So? Maybe he wanted to have a nice little game before dinner," Ace says caustically.

"Yes, maybe. But this is also a sign. It's the sign of the jaguar. See, all their games had religious meanings. This central square here," he says pointing his toe to the place where the four arms cross, "is the jaguar's chamber. And the four arms represent the four gods of the heavens who guarded the chamber...maize, blood, water and light."

"Like the four guardian temples," you suggest.

"Yeah. See, it's oriented in the directions of the compass, the four corners of the earth...north, south, east, west."

"Big deal," Ace theorizes. "By now probably all the Kryptecs know we're looking for the lost city. So he drew the sign of the jaguar. So what?"

"I don't know. It's strange. Besides, why would he put only one pebble on the board? You usually play with four. Maybe it's a warning of some kind."

"Whatever it is, we'd better get a move on. It's getting late," Ace suggests.

"How'd they play this game?" Dentons asks. "With dice?"

"Dice? No, never! The Kryptecs don't believe in chance. They have one word for guessing, deciding, choosing, betting, taking action, gambling, thinking clearly and making up one's mind. The word is *chal*. According to them, the right way to live and act is to do what the jaguar god intends you to do, to move logically according to the rules of the puzzle world...according to *chal*. They have a saying, 'Everything that is, is as it is.'"

"Clever people," Ace concludes.

When you have finished staring stupidly at the game board, you all grab your rifles and head out to search for Manero. An hour or so later, having walked in a large circular path three miles from your encampment, you hear voices through the leaves. Pancho peers silently through the foliage and, standing stiffly behind him, you see another camp with tents, a fire and a handful of armed men lounging, cackling and spitting.

"That them?" Pancho asks quietly.

"Yes, that's them all right. And a meaner bunch of cutthroats you couldn't hope to find."

"Who's hoping!" Pancho gulps.

"That short, fat one there," Ace says pointing with the barrel of her rifle, "is Manero. He's wanted for murder in Mexico. The others are just petty crooks, grave robbers and assorted scum. Gambling, that's all they care about. Gambling and drinking."

"And stinking," Pancho adds as he pinches his nostrils.

"Do you think they'll just give us the map?" Dentons whispers.

"*Give* it to us? Never. Manero may be short, fat and ugly but he's no prince. If they really do have a map showing the location of the guardian temples, they might gamble with us for it, if the stakes are high enough. Sling your rifles and let *me* do the talking," she says as she steps from behind the jungle cover and marches directly into Manero's camp.

You do as she says with the rifle but you also get a tighter grip on your Cracker Jack, the end of which is sticking out of your back pocket. Pancho notices the move and gives you a strange look. As the three of you approach behind Ace, you can see Manero's associates more clearly. All are wearing bulletbelts and carrying long machetes. A handful of grisly faces turn in your direction, faces made even more gruesome by the late afternoon light.

"*Hola, está Manero contigo?*" Ace shouts from a few yards away.

The men scramble for their knives and rifles and soon six gunbarrels are pointing at your quivering lower lip. A large gulp lodges in your throat and refuses to be swallowed.

"Steady," Ace whispers and then says in a louder voice, "*Donde está mi amigo Manero?*"

"*No te acercas! Quédate allá!*"

"It's Ace Kennedy. Tell him it's Ace Kennedy. *Dile que todavia me debe* fifty dollars."

The guns are lowered as the leader—the grubbiest of the whole pack—steps forth. He looks over your group, scratches his stubble, then breaks into a snaggle-toothed laugh. He turns back, shouts to his comrades, conducts a lengthy discussion in Spanish with Ace, then beckons the four of you forward. His motley crew take their places around a freshly started fire. You sit down as well and decide to decline the offer of coffee, the color of bile in a grungy tin cup.

"So, eets true. My old friend Ace Kennedy hez returned. De only woman who hez ever said 'no' to Manero. You hev thought much of theez and changed your mind, sí?"

"That'll be the day, Manero. Keep dreaming. I see you and

your cellmates are still the great fans of bathing you've always been."

"Ella piensa que tenemos mal odor," Manero says turning back to his troops and pointing at his armpits. The mongrels collapse into hysteria.

"We want some information, Manero. Folks around here say you have a map that shows the location of the guardian temples of the lost city of Pixtox. Is that true?"

"So…" he says lighting up the butt of a homemade cigar, "…eets the lost ceety that brings you to Manero. And what would a seemple trader like yourself want to find the great lost ceety for? Heh? For the Gold Jaguar maybe? Sí?"

"No, it's not the lost city itself we're interested in. Or the Gold Jaguar. Everyone knows that's just a fable. Our business is sugar cane. My friends here are looking for a certain type of rare sugar cane."

As if to prove this weak point, you, Pancho and Dr. Dentons simultaneously—and a bit too stiffly—take out your fake ID cards and hold them aloft.

"The natives here say," Ace continues, "that they've seen this sugar cane growing near the guardian temples. But you know the Kryptecs, by the time we get directions out of them…"

"Sugar cane, eh? I theenk you and your nervous friends are looking for a sweeter treasure than that, Señorita. Maybe they are from Mexico Ceety and they wish to take Manero's head back to Mexico in a sugar jar, eh? Heh, heh heh, heh heh heh…"

The entire group of thieves breaks into Manero's form of shotgun laughter. An unsavory bunch, you remark to yourself while outwardly grinning; each one of them is missing equal parts of teeth, manners and couth.

"Keep your head, Manero. We want the map. Do you have it?"

"Perhaps I do, *mi calabaza*. But thees kind of thing can be very expensive. Thees is the secret map of the Kryptec tribe, the only one of eet's kind. Very, very expensive. Perhaps eet is too much to pay for your sugar-loving friends. Eh? Heh, heh heh, heh heh heh…"

Manero launches into another one of his bouts of laughter that is part stutter, part growl. As usual, the morons behind him join in, ignorant of the reason for their own hysterics.

"Well?" Ace demands.

"Sure, Ace, sure. We know where ees thees guardian temples. We been dere many times. We go dere all the time to take peez."

"Peas? You take peas from the guardian temples?"

"Heh, heh heh. No, no, you know…," Manero gets up and makes the familiar gesture of unzipping his fly and relieving himself. His group breaks into applause.

"Look, what do you want for the map?" Ace says in disgust.

Suddenly turning serious, Manero huddles with his men on the far side of the fire, which is now blazing in the twilight. There are shouts, angry glances and slimy smiles before he turns back to your group and addresses Ace.

"Okay, Señorita, maybe we strike the bargain weeth you. We do hev such a map but eets no good to us. Maybe eets no good to you either."

"We'll decide that for ourselves."

"Okay. Then maybe we play the leetle game of chance and we make the deal. Sí?"

"You're too good to me, Manero."

"Manero, he has the good memory," he says poking his fat head with a chubby finger. "Manero does not forget the poker game three years ago when he almost won Ace Kennedy for hees wife."

"Except for my full house."

"Thees one here, the one weeth the nervous eyes," he says pointing to Dr. Dentons, "he eez a gambler? Heh, heh heh. Here is the deal. He plays our leetle game. If he weens, you get the precious map."

"And if he loses?"

"Eef he loses, then the Señorita, she must stay weeth us here for the night. Heh, heh heh, heh heh heh…"

"Yuck!"

"Forget it, Ace," Dr. Dentons says grabbing her by the arm, "let's get out of here. This isn't getting us anywhere."

"No, wait a minute. This map may be our only shot. It's worth a try. If you lose, we can always try to run for it. They won't chase us into the jungle, I don't think. All right," she says turning back to His Ugliness, "you're on, Manero."

Pancho, Ace and you stand up, rifles on your shoulders, ready to make a mad dash. Dr. Dentons moves forward to face

Manero. The others huddle closer as well. One of Manero's men produces two scraps of paper. Manero scribbles something on each of them, folds each of the scraps identically and places them on the ground before Dr. Dentons.

"Be careful, Doc," Pancho whispers, "remember, they're crooks. They always cheat."

Dr. Dentons stares at the two pieces of paper as Manero guzzles whiskey, chews his butt and explains the game.

"Eets really very seemple, my friend. One piece of paper hez the word 'win' written on it. The other hez the word 'lose.' You must peeck one of them. Eef you peeck 'win' Manero gives you the map. But eef you peeck 'lose'…" Manero gives Ace a lecherous grin.

Even though the evening chill is beginning to set in, Dr. Dentons' face is ringed with sweat. He stares at the two pieces of paper as glances shoot back and forth around the fire and logs sputter in the blaze. Suddenly Dr. Dentons looks up, gazes at Manero and grins broadly. Manero, caught off guard, grins back; memories of teeth gleam in the firelight. Dentons reaches down, grabs the folded piece of paper on the right, opens it, then says aloud, "Looks like we've won, Manero," and throws the paper into the fire.

A great ruckus develops as the bandits shout in disbelief. Before they can do anything, Dr. Dentons picks up the other scrap of paper, opens it and displays it to the group. Sure enough, the word "lose" is written on it and the anger subsides. Manero, looking disgusted, throws his cigar butt into the fire.

"Okay, okay. Give heem the map, Imbecilio. Heh, heh heh. Good luck weeth it, my friends, I theenk you'll need it, eh? Thees map is no good to men like us, Ace, but maybe these *sugaristas* of yours can use it. Maybe we'll see you later in the jaguar's chamber, eh? Heh, heh heh, heh heh heh…"

You return to your camp with the map tucked safely under your arm.

"Do you think Manero really knows where the guardian temples are?" Dentons asks Ace. "Or the lost city?"

"Pure bluff. I know him. In that poker game he was trying to bluff my full house with a pair of sevens. He's a born loser."

"Still, it was pretty lucky that you guessed the right piece of paper," you say to Dr. Dentons.

"Luck had absolutely nothing to do with it," he answers. "It was logic, not luck at all."

You gather wood for a fire and try to figure out what he means by that.

"It's really quite simple," Dr. Dentons explains as he zips himself into his sleeping bag. "You see, Manero's a cheat, like Pancho said. I simply assumed that he *always* cheats. The stakes were certainly high enough. Well, that could only mean one thing...and that's what I took advantage of. See? Logic."

And with that the professor rolls over in his cocoon and goes to sleep.

The next day, the irritated squawk of a bright green quetzal seems to sum up the feelings of the group. It becomes quite clear why Manero couldn't use the map and was willing to gamble it away. Although it is neatly drawn and the directions are in simple English, it is completely incomprehensible. As always, as soon as the situation turns puzzling, the others leave the matter in your hands. So, once again, you make yourself comfortable on a rock, and start figuring. *Chal*...as the Kryptecs would say.

In addition to the four instructions, two other facts are clear. The guardian temples are near one of the points of interest on the map, except for the camp. Manero had set up his camp at the precise location shown on the map and there were no temples in sight. You know, too, that the temples are not near any of the clearings because if they were, they wouldn't be clearings, as Pancho points out with Kryptec logic. That leaves seven possible locations. You take out your trusty pencil and get to work.

Turn to the map, page 62.

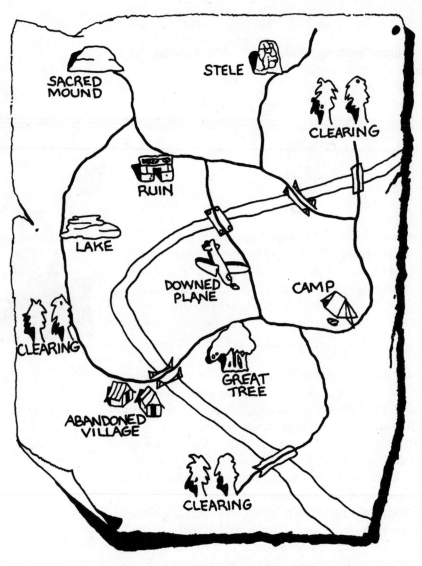

DIRECTIONS TO THE GUARDIAN TEMPLES

1. From the camp, there is a route to the temples that crosses exactly one bridge.

2. From the clearing that is closest to the temples, there is a path to the temples that crosses either one bridge or no bridges.

3. In taking the most direct route to the temples from the clearing that is farthest from the temples, you come to at least one intersection after passing the ruin.

4. If the temples are near the lake, there is a path from them back to the camp that crosses only one intersection.

Despite the convoluted wording and the buzzing mosquitoes, you eventually arrive at a solution. You go through your explanation, but only Dr. Dentons seems to have the patience to follow it. He is about to repeat the instructions to Ace but she quickly interrupts.

"All right, so we have to go up north. This map is a little misleading, though. It's not as close as it looks. The best way to get there is to take the Oozo for a few miles. That'll cut down our travel time. We'll have to go back to the village and hire some canoes. Pancho, do you remember your way back to that village?"

"Sure, I think so. Go straight until you're stifling, then make a left at the big green leaf…"

"Good. In that case, the professor and I will break camp here while you go and get the canoes. That'll save us some time. And don't pay more than five American dollars for them." Then turning to you she adds, "I don't know if you're better off going with Pancho or staying here to help us. What do you think?"

If you decide to go with Pancho to get canoes, read on.
If you decide to stay and wait for his return, turn to page 69.

The village is quiet and mostly empty. The women have left to gather food. Three men are sitting around a smoldering fire playing homemade instruments; the first person is banging a flat drum, the second blows on a bamboo flute and the third is clapping two sticks together.

"Eerie sound," you say as the melody coils through the air.

"Yeah, those are ancient Kryptec instruments. That one there is a Tom, you know, like a tomtom. And the sticks are called Dik, I guess because of the sound they make. The flute is a Haree, basically just a whistle with two holes. Sounds nice, huh?"

Pancho steps over to the group, conducts a short conversation with one of the men, then motions to you to follow him into one of the huts. Inside, another man is sitting in the shadow with his legs crossed. In response to Pancho's question about canoes, he produces a round piece of paper, painted with Kryptec symbols, with a hole in the center. It resembles a paper necklace for a baby's neck.

"He's got canoes all right, and he is willing to sell them to us but only if you can solve this puzzle. It's called Macuilzochitl's Necklace."

"I've seen that design before," you say.

"Yeah...well, it's pretty common. It's part of their calendar. See, Macuilzochitl was..."

"The god of games."

"That's right! One of the jaguar's two sons. Supposedly, Macuilzochitl made this necklace when his own son was a baby. When the boy grew up, the only way he could take his father's place was to wear the necklace, but by then his head and neck were too big. How could he wear it around his neck without breaking the sacred ring?"

"I give up, how could he?"

"No, amigo, *you* have to solve the problem," he says handing you a razor blade. "You have to cut this paper necklace in such a way that you can put it over your head and around your neck. But you cannot cut all the way through the ring. *Comprende?*"

You *comprende* fine, the only problem is that you can't figure out how to do it. You stand there for a long time frowning at the paper ring and at the razor blade. There doesn't seem to be any way to expand the size of the ring without cutting through it. Pancho observes your confusion and offers some words of advice.

"You know, there's a nice word in Kryptec—*tlik*—which means 'to achieve something by waiting around and ignoring it.' Maybe we should have something to eat."

After a snack of nuts, *zaca* and thick coffee, you return to the problem of the ring. As the sounds of the musical instruments whistle through the leaves, you try to think about what kind of cuts you can make in the paper that will somehow increase its size.

Cut out the necklace on the previous page and try to solve the puzzle.

The answer comes in a flash. It was simply the circular shape that was throwing you off. Imagine that the problem was to cut a strip of paper so that it could be stretched, you say to yourself. It's the same problem but easier to visualize. A few quick cuts and you show your solution to the Indian. He is unmoved by your ingenuity. However, true to his word, he makes a deal with Pancho for two canoes. When he is finished, you follow Pancho's wide form through the great leaves.

"That was true *chal,* my friend, it seemed like the answer came to you suddenly. You were in tune with the jaguar."

"He didn't seem too impressed. In fact, none of the Kryptecs ever seem to get too excited about anything."

"That's because they're in perfect harmony with the puzzle world, which is the timeless world of the gods. They're just not caught up in our modern, hectic sense of time. In fact, the Kryptecs have no way to show time. Like the Mayans, they don't differentiate between past and future."

"So how do they tell if something once happened, will happen or is yet to happen..."

"They don't. It doesn't matter to them. Their verbs only have one form. Take their word *plic,* for example. *Plic* means—I used to laugh, I was laughing, I'm always laughing, I will laugh..."

Pancho's words trail off. You're beginning to get a feeling for the intricacies of the Kryptec mind, beginning in fact to believe in the puzzle world. After all, isn't that what modern physicists describe—an intricately designed universe ready to be deciphered by the creative mind? A world of mathematical jigsaws of time and space, open to flashes of insight? The images and sounds of the jungle—secret codes of their own—surround you as you follow Pancho deeper into the mysteries, all the while accompanied by the distant lilting music of the sacred Kryptec instruments...the Tom, Dik and Haree?

5

The Guardian Temples

Catching up with Ace and Dr. Dentons, Pancho explains that he has been given directions to a point nearby at the river's edge where the canoes will be waiting. Although suspicious of the plan, Ace has no choice but to go along with it. You shoulder your backpacks and trudge down to the Oozo.

"We've got to be real careful on this river," Pancho says as he twangs a branch into your face, "there're supposed to be piranha in it."

"There are no piranha here," Dr. Dentons corrects. "They're native to the Amazon River."

"I'm telling you, Doc, they might not be called piranha but they still chew on your toes. Hey, there they are!"

"The piranha?" you gasp.

Following Pancho's finger you notice—half floating, half stuck in the muck—two sorry-looking canoes made out of twigs. They are narrow, curved up at the ends, covered with slime and gashed in the wrong places.

"What on earth are those things?" Dr. Dentons asks.

"Uh...I think those are the *caballitos* we just bought, Doc."

"No kidding. What does the word *caballito* mean...practical joke?"

"Relax, Professor," Ace says, "they're just simple reed boats. The Indians use them all the time to navigate the Oozo. They're not exactly from the Boat Show. They're *supposed* to look homemade."

"You're telling me! Well, I guess if I survived Bimbo I'll survive this," he says and throws his pack into the nearer one with a jaunty heft.

Pancho has a bit more trouble balancing his ample girth in the narrow boat, but he soon settles down at the helm of the other one. "Well, there's a saying," he announces. "When in Tortilla…"

"…learn how to dodge piranha," Ace adds and pushes off from the shore.

You all navigate down the Oozo. The few rays of light that penetrate the thick upper growths are razor-sharp and stark as moonlight. There is no breeze and the sweat pours down your body. All around are decaying leaves and dead trees, remnants of eons of rot. And then, if the barbs and tangles of the jungle don't defeat you, there are the monstrous snakes, the stinging ants, flesh-eating fish and huge mosquitoes. Every morning you have tried to remember to check your boots for scorpions and your water cup for wasps. As you pole along the thin waterway, you can see the fish below baring their teeth and sizing you up for lunch. You vow never to have another tuna sandwich again and hope your promise has penetrated the green slime.

Yet somehow in the midst of all this, the Kryptecs and hundreds of other Indian tribes were able to conquer the jungle and carve glorious civilizations out of it. The Kryptecs especially saw in this sinking morass

something holy... a sacred game. As you slowly pole your way
from no place to nowhere through the steamy heat, you realize
that the greatest puzzle of all is how on earth mankind survives
and thrives.

After a while, Ace motions from the front boat that you have
reached the right spot on the river. You pull the *caballitos* up
onto the riverbank, turn them over, and cover them with leaves.
  "Listen," Ace says, "if we get separated for any reason..."
  "Separated?" Dentons jumps.
  "If anything happens, memorize the location of these boats
near the foot of this huge tree," she says pointing to one tree
that towers above the rest. "If you take this river downstream for
another eight miles, you'll be back at the landing strip where we
left the plane. I think you can see Bimbo from the river. That is,
if she hasn't been stolen."
  "And if she has been stolen?"
  "Learn to speak Kryptec."
You hike a few more miles through the heat to the area
indicated on the map where the guardian temples are to be
found. The Sacred Mound is a large bump in a clearing. A quick
survey of the area shows that it is surrounded by the four
temples, about a mile apart from each other, each shrouded by
the jungle.
  "These must be them," Pancho says taking out his compass.
"They're laid out exactly according to the four points of the
compass. Now the question is... which one points to the lost
city?"
  Dentons takes out the poem and reads it aloud.

" 'Come to me when my tallest son will point the way at a temple's point; then step into the mouth of _____ and come to my secret chamber.' It seems to me this must be referring to the tallest temple."

"Okay, but how do we know which temple that is, since we can't see any one from any of the others to compare them? Hey, you're the riddle expert," Pancho says turning to you, "which one do we pick?"

You begin to feel that your role as a—what did Mac call it, heuristist?—is starting to be abused, that the others might be using you to make decisions for them. On the other hand, someone has to decide how to proceed, so you take on the responsibility. Realizing that there isn't enough information to make a rational choice, you make a totally random guess about which temple to try—North, South, East, West. But, of course, when you make your choice known, you try to say it with the kind of firm tone that suggests a great deal of clever thinking.

If you decide to try the north temple, turn to page 73.
If you decide to try the south temple, turn to page 77.
If you decide to try the east temple, turn to page 80.
If you decide to try the west temple, turn to page 82.

You all proceed to the north temple. It seems to be the shortest of the four and from that point of view the least promising. But you decide to stand by your intuition and give it a try. The four of you leave all your equipment outside at the base of the steps, walk up the narrow stone slabs, step through the entranceway and enter a wide, low room. Three of the walls are plain and empty but the far one is covered with an elaborate carving, a series of identical panels.

"Definitely Kryptec," Dentons muses.

"Probably another one of their puzzle patterns," Pancho says, focusing his flashlight on the wall.

"What kind of puzzle pattern?" you ask.

"I've seen designs like this before. Usually one of the panels is...hey, what's that sound?"

Suddenly you notice that there is a grinding sound coming from somewhere in the temple. You turn automatically toward the entrance but it is too late. An enormous stone block has moved into place, completely cutting off your exit. You are trapped inside the room. Flashlights desperately search the darkness. Panic takes over, but no amount of struggle can budge the stone door. There doesn't seem to be any other way out either. The stones in the walls have been fitted with airtight precision. You try to suggest, with a calm voice, that everyone sit down and analyze the situation but you no sooner get the appeal out of your mouth than you hear a small explosion. From a hidden duct, water comes gushing into the room. In no time at all you are up to your knees in the flood.

"There *must* be some way out of here!" you shout—half insisting, half pleading. "There must be a way to drain the water out! Look for some kind of drain."

You grope frantically in the murky water. But the floor seems to be solid and smooth. Meanwhile, the level of the tide rises swiftly.

"No, wait a minute!" Pancho shouts. "I bet it's the wall!"

"What's the wall?"

"The wall is the way out. It's a Kryptec puzzle. One of the

panels must be different from the others. I bet if we can find that panel and move it, the water will stop."

"Well, which one is it?"

"I can't tell, can you?"

Everyone is already beginning to tread water, but somehow all flashlights are directed at the panels. Time is running out. You must quickly find the one panel that is different from the others.

"I see it!" you shout but you are too far away to swim to it in time. Pancho and Dr. Dentons are much closer. "Can't you see the one, Pancho? Squint at it! Squint!"

"Yes, I see it. Come on, Doc...*Push!*"

Their efforts alone don't work. By the time you and Ace swim over, the panel is half submerged. It's hard to get leverage while bobbing in the pool.

"Hurry! *Push!*"

"It's no use!"

"Try again," Ace commands. "One...two...glub..."

The stone moves. You try one more time, in unison, and it moves a bit farther. On the third underwater heave the stone slides out of its niche and plops out on the far side of the temple wall. Fresh air rushes into the room and sunlight teases from the other side of the window as the water pours through the gap at the level of the missing stone. One by one you climb through the opening and ride the stream to freedom.

Outside the temple, panting and drying off in the burning sun, Ace says, "Why'd you tell Pancho to squint at the wall?"

"Squinting makes it easier to see whole patterns. It eliminates the details," you say, wringing your socks.

"I don't think the Kryptecs actually want us to find their lost city," Ace says.

"Why?" Pancho demands slightly offended. "This is probably just one of the tricks their ancestors built to protect Pixtox. They didn't tell us *which* of the four temples was the right one, and the other three are probably traps."

"You think this water trap is ancient?"

"Could be," Dentons answers. "It could be a sand-operated gizmo that diverts water from a cistern…"

"I'm telling you, Ace, they're helping us the only way they can … by showing us the puzzles and letting us find our own way. Maybe Manero's the one we should be afraid of. What if *he* killed that Indian, did you ever think of that?"

"He's too stupid," Ace answers.

"You know," Dr. Dentons says, gazing back in the direction of the Oozo, "I'm really beginning to hate water."

"Why, Doc?" Pancho asks shaking his ear. "It's like the Kryptecs say… if there were no water, we couldn't learn how to swim and then we'd all drown."

To explore the south temple, turn to page 77.
To explore the east temple, turn to page 80.
To explore the west temple, turn to page 82.

The south temple contains four rooms, all quite narrow, connected by stone doorways. As usual, since there are no windows, it is pitch-dark inside and you are forced to rely on flashlights. The rooms are empty, but in the corner on the floor of one of them you find some scraps of paper. They look like they might fit together somehow and you get to work. Shoving the flashlight under your chin, you try to keep the beam on the pieces while you juggle the jigsaw. Meanwhile, Ace and Pancho leave to explore the outside of the building. You turn the scraps this way and that, trying to see the whole.

"Any luck?" Dr. Dentons asks.

Cut out the pieces above and try to solve the jigsaw.

When you have correctly placed the last piece, it becomes clear that this is a section of a larger piece of paper that has been torn up. It is a chart of some kind but its contents still remain a mystery.

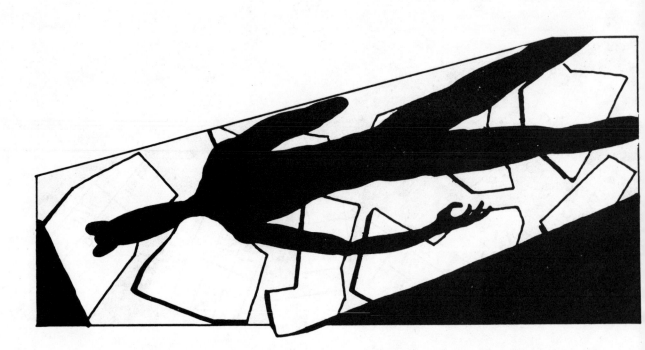

"What was that?" Dentons wonders, responding to a muffled sound coming from one of the other rooms.

Your back is to the darkness but you dare not turn around. Slowly you remove the flashlight from under your chin and direct it toward the doorway. Dentons looks at you, then at the door, and the sound comes again, like a low clatter. He takes out his pistol, places his flashlight on the floor and moves stiffly and silently into the adjoining chamber. One step into the doorway and there is a loud squawk, a frenzy of fluff and feathers. Dentons jumps back and a large chicken bounds into the room, races twice around the perimeter and darts out the front entrance.

"Chicken," Dentons says dusting off his pants and regaining his composure. "Didn't see him before."

You laugh. He laughs. You stare back down at the paper scraps trying to see the clue, if any, that they offer. You stand up, turn around. Dentons is standing in front of you, framed by the doorway.

Suddenly a shadow looms behind Dentons. A figure prepares to pounce. You gasp, dive for your Cracker Jack but Dentons is faster. He wheels about, raises his gun and shoots. He catches the jaguar in mid-leap. It twists over in the air and comes crashing to the floor. Pancho and Ace come running, rifles cocked, but by the time they tumble into the room, the excitement is over. Lying in the dirt at your feet is the lifeless form of a man in a jaguar costume.

"Good God!" Dentons cries. "I've never shot anyone before!"

"I wouldn't feel too bad about it if I were you," Ace says. "Look at those claws. He could have ripped you to shreds."

"He who?" Pancho asks, but an examination of the body reveals no identification whatsoever. "Well, he sure isn't an Indian," Pancho continues, "he doesn't even look Hispanic."

Pancho is right. He is a tall, thin man with a fair complexion. You notice that his shoes are covered with black goo.

"Should we go and report this?" Dentons asks no one in particular.

"No way," Ace answers. "We can't get involved with the authorities. Besides, I have the distinct feeling we're running out of time."

"And luck," Pancho adds.

"We'd better move on to the next temple."

"And just leave him here?" Dentons says with a wince.

"We either leave him here...or join him. Let's get going."

"Hey," Pancho says, "I wonder if he's one of these assassins?"

"Not any more."

"You know that Indian that was killed two days ago? He said something about assassins. I wonder if he meant him. Maybe there are more of them around."

"I've got a great idea," Ace says heading for the door. "Let's *not* stay to find out."

To explore the north temple, turn to page 73.
To explore the east temple, turn to page 80.
To explore the west temple, turn to page 82.

At the east temple, you climb the tall flight of stone steps to reach the chamber inside. The feeling that you are being followed—by silent Kryptecs, eternal demons, a band of assassins—is growing and so, while you, Pancho and Ace investigate the temple itself, Dr. Dentons stands guard at the base. Ace takes up a position outside the front door as you and Pancho enter cautiously.

You stand in the middle of the room. Here there is ample light coming in from openings in the wall. Pancho is leaning against one of the walls of the room, his elbow propped on the stone. He looks bored, no doubt waiting for you to make some great discovery, you decide. You look around but there is nothing unusual besides some strange patterns carved into the walls. Suddenly Pancho leaps in the air and shouts.

"Madre de Dios! Let's get out of here!"

Without knowing what it is you're escaping, you make a dash for the entrance and jump through the doorway after him. As you pass through the portal, the sound of a thundering crash gives you an extra push. Outside, you plow into Ace and almost knock her down the massive steps. A thick cloud of dust billows from the exit.

When the dust settles, you return to the room with Pancho to discover that a large section of the roof has collapsed. Huge stones have crashed to the floor, completely burying the shadow you left behind in a panic.

"How the hell did you know *that* was going to happen?" you ask Pancho in disbelief.

"I knew *something* bad was going to happen. It's that carving on the wall. See what it is?"

At first you can't quite make it out; it seems to be just a collection of wavy lines. But then you go up to the spot where Pancho was standing. There, very close to the right-hand edge of the carving, the image becomes terrifyingly clear.

"Everybody knows that symbol," Pancho says, "but to the Kryptecs it meant certain death. This place is booby-trapped and we were almost the boobies who were trapped."

On the way down the temple steps, Pancho, trying to calm his own nerves, keeps up the chatter. "You know, amigo, I'm beginning to feel a little bit like Nononatuagen."

"Who's that?" you ask still shuddering.

"Nononatuagen was the great unwanted god of Central America. In Indian mythology, Nononatuagen took human form and used to show up at all the ritual feasts and eat all the food. Every time he appeared, the people used to jump up and shout *No no not you again!*"

Then, noticing that you're not joining him in a frail cackle, Pancho adds, "That's just a little Aztec humor there, kemosabe."

"Very little," you assess.

 To try the north temple, turn to page 73.
To try the south temple, turn to page 77.
To try the west temple, turn to page 82.

The west temple is the most impressive of the ruins, towering above the vegetation. As a group, looking cautiously in all directions, you climb the steep steps to the main chamber. Stones dislodged by your footsteps tumble down to earth as if falling off a mountain.

Inside the room at the top of the structure you find nothing but the usual dirt floor, stone walls and moss. The bright sun outside barely leaks in through the cracks in the wall.

"Well, now for the really big puzzle. What do we do now that we're here?" Pancho wonders sitting down on the floor.

"I guess we wait for the temple to point the way at its point...or something," Dr. Dentons quotes as he too collapses to the dirt.

"'...my tallest son will point the way at a temple's point,'" Ace says reading from the poem. "Do you have any idea what to do?" she asks you.

You don't.

"You know, amigo, there are many ways to solve a problem," Pancho says trying to fill the pause with some philosophy. "Don't worry, the answer will come to you. I have faith in you. The Kryptecs have dozens of words meaning 'to solve.'"

"Naturally."

"*Chalta* means 'to solve something easily.' *Tlan* means 'to solve with difficulty,' *tatln* means 'to solve after years of hardship,' *xicla* means 'to solve by getting the answer from someone else' and *nonchitla* means 'to solve by giving up'..."

"There's a fine idea," Ace says with a grump.

"Of course, those words also mean 'to make an easy decision,' 'to struggle with,' 'to devote one's life to,' 'to form a conspiracy'

and 'to accept death.' Then, of course, depending on the context..."

"Spare us the wretched details, Pancho," Ace insists rubbing her head. "What time is it anyway?"

"Noon."

Just then, as if the word itself had some kind of magical power, the room is transformed. A shaft of light suddenly appears from the ceiling, creating a bright spot in the middle of the floor.

"Holy *xit,* as the Kryptecs say," Pancho exclaims, "where'd that come from?"

"It's noon. The sun is directly overhead," Dentons says squinting toward the ceiling. "There must be a shaft up there that's hidden in darkness until exactly noon."

"When the *sun* is tallest," you shout. "Didn't Pancho say that the sun is one of the jaguar's two sons?"

"Of course that's it! My tallest *sun* will point the way...at a temple's point. The roof?"

"Let's find out."

The opening into the shaft is narrow and this restriction decides your next course of action. Pancho will stay down and boost the three of you up. Once you reach the opening, you see that the arrangement of stones in the shaft forms a series of rungs or ledges that can be used to climb up to the top. The sun is directly above, bathing you in light, as you climb up through the moist rocks. When all three of you have reached the summit, you stand up, turn around and gaze in awe.

There, behind the temple, in a valley in the jungle masked all around by high vegetation, is the lost city of Pixtox.

"I can't believe it," Dr. Dentons says, "we've really found it! That's got to be it!"

"That's it all right," Ace agrees. "You can't see it from any other point but this because it's hidden in that valley."

"Hey, what's going on?" Pancho yells from below.

"We found Pixtox," you shout down to him. "It's right behind the temple in a valley." Standing in the spotlight below, like a dancer on a stage, you see Pancho give a rotund little jump for joy. Then turning back to Pixtox, you get a sudden insight.

"The *west* temple. I should have known," you say.

"Why?"

"That patolli board back at the camp. It only had one pebble on it, remember? That pebble was on the western arm. It was a hint."

"From whom?"

"Must've been the guide. Maybe that was the only way he could tell us which was the right temple."

You pass the binoculars back and forth, admiring the fortress that stretches out before you.

"It's hard to believe that a city of this size could stay lost," you say. "Do you really think Manero ever got here?"

"I doubt it. He's usually too drunk to know *where* he is."

"Imagine...lost for all these centuries!"

"Look," Ace says adjusting the focus for a better view, "nothing that's been lost is hard to find...if you know just where to look for it."

"You're beginning to sound like a Kryptec," Pancho shouts from the depths.

"AARGH!" Dentons howls.

"What do you mean 'aargh'?" you quip.

But Dentons isn't kidding. He has taken a few jumpy steps and collapsed, holding his thigh in pain. A sound whizzes past your ear. Assuming that he has been nipped by a large insect, you try to swat it away. But others swoop near. Then you realize that they aren't insects at all...they're darts. You are under attack from somewhere below. You hit the rocks. Ace, acting quickly, leaps behind one of the stones and fires. There are shouts in the jungle. A scream. The darts stop.

"I think I got him," she says. She pulls the dart out of Dentons' leg, takes her long jungle knife and—before he can protest—cuts an X in the wound. *"You,"* she says meaning no one but yourself, "suck out the wound."

"Hah? Me?" you ask.

"Hurry up, it's poison. *And don't swallow!*" Then she disappears down the shaft.

You do as she says, drawing the fluid out of the cut and spitting it out. When Ace returns to the roof, she bandages the leg, attaches a tourniquet just above the wound and ties a rope around Dentons' chest to lower him down the shaft. By the time you finish maneuvering him down the tunnel, and climbing

down yourself, you're exhausted and drenched with sweat. Unfortunately, however, there is no time for a nice nap and shower.

"Oorara?" Pancho asks.

"Probably. It didn't go in too deep," Ace answers.

"Oorara?" you repeat mindlessly.

"It's a poison, a form of strychnine. Look, I've got to go back to the river and kill a coati."

"That's great, I'll get the white bread and the mayonnaise," you say trying to join the fun.

"A coati's a kind of raccoon. Its blood is the best antidote and cure for this kind of poison. If I can find one right away, the professor will be all right by tomorrow. But we don't have much time. Whoever's after us is closing in. Pancho, you stay here and guard Dentons. That means it's up to you to get into the lost city and find the jaguar," she says to you.

You try to think of a retort, an excuse, an alternative plan— but none come to mind. You know she's right. You are the only one who can find the way through the maze of Pixtox and solve the remaining puzzles you're sure to find. And besides, you aren't about to go out and kill the coati instead.

"All right," you say with fake bravura, "you can count on me. It's a far, far better thing I do now than I ever thought I could be talked into. Just one question: What am I looking for?"

"The Gold Jaguar."

"I know *that*. But I mean...where is it?"

"Brave youth!" Dentons mumbles groggily. "Remember the legend. Find your way through the maze to the center of the city. There's a tall building there with three doors. That's the Temple of the Jaguar. If it's like most of these temples, there's a room inside that's the initiation chamber. Maybe the jaguar's in there."

"But what about the last part of the poem? Step into the mouth of...the mouth of what?"

"We won't know that until we find the missing word. Forget it for now. Maybe it's not important. Good luck."

"And for heaven's sake...*hurry!*" Ace says.

"Leave heaven to the gods," Pancho corrects, "and hurry for *our* sakes."

6

The Lost City

For the sake of speed, you leave all your belongings at the foot of the west temple with Pancho and Dr. Dentons. You take only your Cracker Jack, pad and pencil, flashlight, and as much courage as you can scrape hastily together. You pick your way down the hill behind the temple. After you have scrambled about a quarter of a mile—sliding down the decline, stepping over vines and rotting trunks, pushing aside gargantuan leaves— suddenly, as if emerging from an eerie mist, the two gates to the lost city loom before you. Without a map, there is no clue about which way to enter. A great stone labyrinth stretches ahead and you have an uneasy sense that the entire mission rests on your ability to get through the maze to The Temple of the Jaguar. Can you do it? Can you find your way from one of the entrances through the maze of rooms to the tall tower with three doors in the center of the city?

Turn to page 88 and find your way through the maze.

The Lost City

What seems like an eternity passes as you follow your instincts—or is it simply *chal*—through the left gate and the first stone portal, then up and down ancient steps, under arches and across walkways until, exhausted and dizzy from the twists and turns, you find yourself standing next to the stele in the yard before the tower. You wipe the sweat from your forehead, try to gulp down your fears, and proceed hesitantly up the steps. From this new height you gaze around. The city seems completely empty, populated only by rats, broken relics, ancient shadows and forgotten myths. You walk into the central door and enter another of the dark, wet rooms you have come to expect from the Kryptec architects. This must be the initiation chamber, you say to the echo. Here, you search high and low but the only item in the room is a single carving on one of the walls. It is a very ornate sculpture of a human head with an elaborate headdress. You recognize the face—it is Macuilzochitl, son of the jaguar, playing more games with your fate.

You're not quite sure what to do next. What exactly are you looking for anyway? If Pancho were here, he would tell you to think like a Kryptec. You give it a try. What would you *expect* to find in the initiation chamber, if you were a Kryptec? A hidden

image of the jaguar, of course! So, flashlight in hand, you probe the convoluted carvings of the head, searching for a hidden jaguar.

 *See the carving on page 90.*

"Aha!" you shout practically standing on your head. "There it is! This is the right place all right. Now what?"

Scores of questions tumble from your throbbing brain. What to do? Look for the 'mouth of' something, as it says in the poem? Find a hidden doorway? Wait until noon? Or just assume that the entire expedition has led to this dreary dead end?

The combined effects of the heat and damp seem about to defeat you. The air feels heavy and thick. Your own temples start to pound. You sit down opposite the stone carving and lean back against the wall. It is strangely warm for rock but you ignore the sensation, tired of riddles and questions. You close your eyes. What was that Kryptec word Pancho told you about? The one that meant solving something by ignoring it. Was it *chal* or *tlic* or *tlan*? You rub your scalp, stuff your flashlight into your waistband and lean back with all your weight.

You're falling backward! Is it a dream? No, the stone has given way as if it were on a hinge. You try to grab the adjacent stones but they are too slippery. Your fingers slide off the moss; you tumble and roll down a slope—a tunnel like a laundry chute— and soon come flying into another room far below the first. You hit the floor hard, fumble with your flashlight, drop it, pick it up, then drop it again. Imagining ghosts, jaguars, bogeymen and maniacs looming in the surrounding blackness, you finally flip the switch on the handle and beam the light in all directions. You are alone.

You seem to have landed in a second chamber perhaps fifty feet below the first. This room has carvings along the upper edges of the walls, jaguar faces on a continuous frieze. The room is locked in antiquity, as if no living soul had entered in hundreds of years. It is a small room, no more than ten feet on each side. On one wall is the square opening through which you made your clumsy entrance.

Then you discover—by tripping over it—something in the center of the floor. It is a low flat stone, about one foot high and two feet on each side. You get down on your knees to examine it further. Leaning conspicuously against it is a small, rather dull and tarnished medallion in the shape of a hexagon. You pick it up, shine your light on it, inspect it carefully. Engraved on its face is the image of a jaguar. Made of a thin sheet of metal, it doesn't seem to be especially valuable. It fits easily into the palm of your hand and can't weigh more than a pound. Even in the direct beam of light it doesn't have a priceless lustre. Can this be the prize you've been seeking? Is this ordinary-looking pendant the great Gold Jaguar for which the Aztecs and Cortez searched? Impossible, you mutter, but you know it must be so. There is nothing else here.

You search the room again, assuming that you've missed something obvious and crucial. But nothing else comes to light. The walls are flat and bare and the carvings near the ceiling look typical and insignificant. The floor is solid. You inspect the stone in the center of the floor. It is flat on top and, probing closer, you notice that a square has been etched onto its top surface. It looks as though a plaque had been removed, leaving only the indentation. But you can't tell whether this is recent or from the remote past. You place the jaguar next to it. The medallion is almost the same size as the indentation but, being hexagonal, it won't fit into it. Around the edges of the stone you now see black smudges that look like fingerprints.

You are stymied. Perhaps the others can make sense of your findings. You put the medallion in your shirt, crouch back through the opening in the wall and clamber back up the incline. In the initiation chamber again, you swing the stone door back in place behind you. It closes smoothly and merges perfectly with the rest of the wall. When you are back outside standing on the steps of the temple, you hear what sounds like rifle fire in the distance. Knowing that things must be heating up for the others, you quickly retrace your steps through the lost city, slip and slash your way through the jungle and return to the base of the west temple.

"Stay down!" Ace orders as you casually stroll out from the far side of the temple. "Pancho? Can you see anything?" she shouts.

"Yeah. They're running back into the bush. There are two of them."

"Only two? Can you see what they look like?"

"Nah, they're too far away."

"Damn!"

You all emerge from your hiding places and gather together in front of the temple, near the backpacks. The ground is littered with darts.

"It's a good thing those guys are lousy with darts. I think they only got the professor before by accident," Ace says surveying the battlefield.

"If they're soldiers working for the generals," Dentons says, "why don't they just shoot us?"

"Whoever it is, they're trying to make it look like they're Kryptecs. But I don't think they are."

"Why not?"

"They're too tall. And the one in the jaguar suit was too blond."

"And there's one other reason we can be sure they're not Kryptecs," Pancho adds.

"What's that?"

"Kryptecs *never* miss."

"What do they do," you ask innocently, "practice all day?"

"No. Kryptecs never miss because they don't decide what the target is until *after* they've hit something," he says smiling.

"Do you think you can walk, Professor?" Ace says pointing to the bandaged leg.

"Look, call me Paul, will you? This 'Professor' business has gone far enough. I can walk all right … but what the devil did you find out?" he inquires turning to you.

"Not now," Ace interjects. "We're not safe here. Let's get back to the canoes and camp there. We can protect ourselves better near the river."

Returning to the Oozo by a different path to avoid being tracked, you set up a new camp a few yards away from the aging boats. Only when you're all settled in do you have a chance to recount your afternoon's adventure. At the climax of your story you pull out the medallion and place it ceremoniously before the group.

"This is *it?*" Ace shouts with rage. "Mac must be out of his mind sending us on this crazy mission. This looks like something they mass-produce for tourists in Mexico City!"

"*El jaguar de oro?* Is this thing even made of gold?" Pancho asks hopefully.

"Let's find out," Dentons says taking a small kit out of his backpack. The kit contains a piece of fabric, a small dark stone and a tiny bottle with an eyedropper. The three of you watch intently as he cleans the medallion with the fabric, rubs one of the corners of the jaguar against the stone, then drops a few beads of the liquid from the bottle on the scratches the jaguar medallion has made on the stone.

"It's a touchstone," Dentons explains noticing everyone's curiosity. "This bottle contains nitric acid, which will chemically interact with the scratches and tell us . . . there, see the color changing? I'd say this medallion is probably ten-karat gold, what's known as tourist's gold." Then, examining the jaguar with a magnifying glass, he continues: "But it's worth less than that because it's not even solid. It's only gold-plated. My friends, this priceless relic for which we have risked our lives was made about a year ago and costs . . . approximately . . . sixty-five dollars."

"Sixty-five dollars?" Pancho groans morosely.

"Give or take."

"Look," Ace says fanning herself with her hat, "let's go over this whole thing again. We're obviously missing something."

As the sun fades over the treetops, you recount your journey to the secret chamber over and over again. You repeat every detail: the architectural maze filled with broken statues, the carving of Macuilzochitl with its hidden jaguar, the secret door, the stone on the ground with the square indentation. But none of it seems to lead anywhere. The Kryptec riddles seem only to be leading you in circles, as if the jaguar god itself were toying with your destinies on a great cosmic patolli board.

In the morning a young boy appears at your encampment. He conducts a brief conversation with Pancho in Spanish, then squats down and stares off serenely toward the river. Pancho returns to the tents and translates.

"That's a new one," he says scratching the back of his neck. "This kid says that Joe Chemilko wants to see us, to talk to us. He says that he's waiting about fifty yards down the riverbank."

"Joe Chemilko? The Joe Chemilko who they named the capital city after?" you ask in confusion.

"I doubt it, amigo. This guy's old, but he's probably not *that* old. Joe Chemilko is a name of respect that's given to village elders. Anybody who has earned the right to be called Joe Chemilko has a great knowledge of tribal lore. He's probably worth talking to. I guess we should go see what's up."

"Could be another ambush," Ace reflects. "On the other hand, if they knew we were here, they could have hit us while we were asleep."

"They who?"

"Anyone."

"Look," Dentons adds, "if this old geezer knows so much about tribal lore maybe he can tell us what this jaguar medallion is for."

Convinced by that possibility, you grab the Gold Jaguar medallion and the poem along with the translation and follow the boy along the swampy edge of the Oozo River. Soon you come upon a man sitting on a chair in the shade of the leaves next to the water. His boat is tied to the roots of a nearby tree. He is indeed quite old and the history of Tortilla seems to be carved into the leathery skin of his face. From his strangely aloof and gentle manner, you know immediately that he is a Kryptec.

Pancho's conversation with him begins in English, switches to Spanish but soon winds up in Kryptec as the talk changes to matters of the Gold Jaguar.

"He says we are in great danger," Pancho explains. "We must stay away from the lost city. The lost city now holds only the secrets of death."

"Why is that?" you ask.

"He says that the jaguar god is angry and is spilling its blood over the land."

"Why is the jaguar god angry?"

"It's angry because men no longer believe in the puzzle world. Even many of the Kryptecs no longer truly believe."

"Ask him if that's why some of his people are trying to kill us," Ace suggests.

"Kryptec'tl?" Pancho asks. ·

"Nic'tloc," the old man replies with a wince.

"He says that's not true at all. His people would never try to kill others. The jaguar god is angry with all men and has sent assassins into the world. It is these assassins who have attacked us. They are tainted with the jaguar's blood and they will kill *anyone* who gets too close to the lost city."

"He said all that?" you ask.

"Yup. I told you, Kryptec is a very compact language."

"That's what the Indian who was killed was trying to tell us. He was trying to warn us about the 'assassins of Macuilzochitl.'"

"Xixitec," the old man interrupts.

"What's he say?" Dentons asks.

"He says that his grandson's brother's son-in-law was murdered the other day because he divulged the secret of how to find the lost city. Macuilzochitl, the jaguar's son, directed the assassins to kill him for that. And now that they know we've found Pixtox, they're going to kill us."

"Wait a minute," Dentons insists. "This routine has gone far enough. How can *xixitec* possibly mean all that? I'm beginning to wonder about you."

"That's what it means, Doc," Pancho answers sounding slightly offended at the mistrust. "The word *xi* is a shorthand for the lost city. *Xixi* means that it was recreated in words...in other words, told to somebody. The way he held his hand up to his mouth when he said it means it was told as a secret. The ending *tec* refers to someone's grandson's brother's son-in-law. Now, the inflection on the second *xi*," Pancho says trying to emphasize the barely audible swallowing of the syllable, "means that someone was killed because of a certain action. But the positions of the words..."

"Never mind!" Dentons shouts, exhausted by the explanation. "I'll never doubt you again!"

"How does he know all this? Ask him that," Ace instructs.

"He says Macuilzochitl came to him in a vision. He was tall and blond and his fingers and boots were dark with the jaguar's blood. He told Joe Chemilko that the jaguar was angry and that no one was to go near the lost city again."

"Show him the medallion and see what he says."

Pancho hands the old man the medallion and translates his response.

"He says this looks like the kind of cheap tourist souvenir they sell in Mexico City. Still, he says he'll buy it from us for a pound of $10 gold pieces or a half pound of $20 gold pieces whichever is..."

"Oh no!" you say, exasperated. "Forget it. Let's see if he can explain the last part of the poem."

Pancho retrieves the Gold Jaguar medallion from the Indian's hand and hands him instead the piece of paper with the Kryptec symbols on it along with your translation. After the old man has had time to look at both, Pancho points to the spot where the word is missing. The Indian shrugs, takes out a pouch of tobacco and begins to roll a cigarette. He and Pancho trade a few more monosyllables.

"Well?"

"He says he has heard this poem before, many years ago. The name that is missing is the jaguar's grandson, one of Macuilzochitl's sons."

"Please, no more sons!"

"Shhh!" Pancho whispers. "He speaks English. You'll insult him. Macuilzochitl's son was the only deity who could speak directly to the jaguar god. He says that's what the expression 'climb into the mouth of' means. You can get to the jaguar god directly via this god. It's *his* name that's missing."

"Well, what *is* the god's name?" Dentons asks.

"It's ineffable. It can't be said out loud."

"So tell him to whisper it."

"No, Ace, you don't understand. He's not permitted to say the name at all. It's a secret name."

Before continuing the interview, you decide to have a conference a few feet away from the old Indian.

"I think we're missing something," Dentons concludes.

"I'd agree with you if I knew what we were trying to find out," Ace says.

"The professor's right," Pancho adds, "I think we've missed something in Pixtox. I don't believe all this jazz about assassins, but somebody sure as hell doesn't want us inside the lost city. Maybe it has some kind of military importance we're not aware of."

"The generals?"

"Maybe."

"I don't know about that," Dentons responds, "but everything sure seems to point back to Pixtox. Maybe we'll have a clue if we can find out the meaning of this last part of the poem, the missing name."

"What'll that do for us?"

"I don't know. Maybe there's an image of this god somewhere inside the lost city. Maybe if you stick your finger in its nose you find a secret passage. Who knows?"

"Secret passage? Where, back to Kansas?"

But in spite of Ace's sarcasm, you realize that no one has any better leads and so you all return to the old man with a new set of questions.

"Ask him what this god looks like," you suggest.

"*Tlul?*" Pancho says.

"*L'can,*" the Indian replies.

"He says he can show us what the god looks like but the only way to summon the image is with the name. He says that, like men, the gods only appear when they are summoned by name."

Catching a faint glint in Joe Chemilko's crinkled eyes and knowing that he seems to want to help, you suggest that he simply write the name down, knowing full well that this leaves you open to the tricks and treats of his religion. The Indian smiles slightly as Pancho translates your suggestion.

"He wants to know what language you want him to write it in."

"English," you say.

The Indian takes a piece of paper from you and pulls out an old stump of a pencil from his jacket. Fingers that have dug in the soil and picked berries for ages carefully inscribe the name on the paper. The parched skin of his knuckles buckles deeply as he flexes his antique bones to write. Smoke from his cigarette stub drifts upward into the thick air.

When he is finished, he hands the paper to Pancho who looks at it momentarily, shakes his head, then gives it to you. Ace and Dr. Dentons peer over your shoulder, exchange confused glances, then back off, leaving you alone with the clue. The paper is inscribed with a series of geometric arrow shapes.

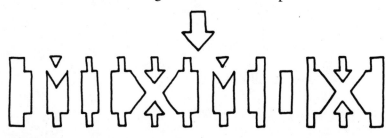

"What are we supposed to do with this?" you ask Pancho.

"That's the name of the god who can speak directly to the jaguar. I guess if you can tell Joe what it says, he can tell us what the god looks like."

"And it's in English?"

"I guess so."

You stare at the paper blankly for a while. You have asked the Indian to write down a name in English and he has complied. The name is there somewhere, but where is it? What is it?

You try looking at it from different angles, holding it up and down, turning it over, craning your neck, squinting. But it's not until, quite by accident, you place one hand along the top edge of the shapes that the name suddenly jumps out. You show it to Pancho.

"Yes, I see it now," Pancho says. "But remember, in Kryptec all x's are pronounced 'sh.'"

The Indian, still silently inhaling his homemade cigarette, peers up at you through the thick cloud of smoke, nods once and takes another piece of paper from his jacket pocket. This one is in the shape of a fan and is covered with wavy lines that don't seem to illustrate anything at all. He fans himself once with the paper, then hands it to you. He summons the boy and, as if the weight of the centuries were on his shoulders, gets up by leaning on the boy's thin frame, drags his chair over to the boat and prepares to leave.

"Ask him if he thinks these assassins want to take over the government," Ace says to Pancho.

"He says," Pancho translates, "that he has already said too much."

"How long has all this been going on?"

"Too long, he says."

"Has he lived here his whole life?"

"He says not yet."

"Well...ask him about the phone booth we found in the jungle, and the meter, and the scraps of paper and..."

But the boat has already drifted to the middle of the river and is being carried downstream, out of earshot, the old man sitting on his chair implacably at the back of the boat.

Back at your camp there are no answers, only more knots to unravel as you review your meeting with Joe Chemilko.

"What was all that stuff about Macuilzochitl coming to him in a vision?"

"Well, look. He's an old *sertanista*. He's supposed to have visions that help him make important decisions about the future of the tribe."

"What's a *sertanista?*" you ask. "Someone who's certain of something?"

"Sort of, gringo," Pancho answers. "It's a Portuguese word meaning someone who's wise in jungle ways. A village elder who knows things."

"Do you think he really believes that these assassins are divine? I wonder if he knows who they really are. The one the professor plugged back at the temple sure went down like flesh and blood."

"Who knows what the old man really knows," Dentons says. "These Kryptecs are so..."

"Cryptic?"

"Exactly."

"And what's that bit about Macuilzochitl being tall and blond with his fingers and boots dark with the jaguar's blood?"

"I have no idea," Pancho says hitting himself in the chin with the fan-shaped paper. "The jaguar god was supposed to have black blood, so I guess that's why their fingers and boots are dark. Well, one thing is clear anyway."

"What's that?"

"I'm confused."

"I've got news for you," Dentons says. "Anyone who comes here and *isn't* confused really doesn't know what the hell is going on!"

"Meanwhile, what about this little item," Pancho says as he flaps the paper in the breeze. "I'm pretty sure it's one of their *tlat,* one of their paper puzzles. But he didn't give us a clue about it. I guess it contains the image of this god Mixmox. Do you know what to do with it, amigo?"

"I know what I'd like to do with it."

"Great, then she's all yours," Ace says and snatches the paper from Pancho's chubby grip and drops it in your hands.

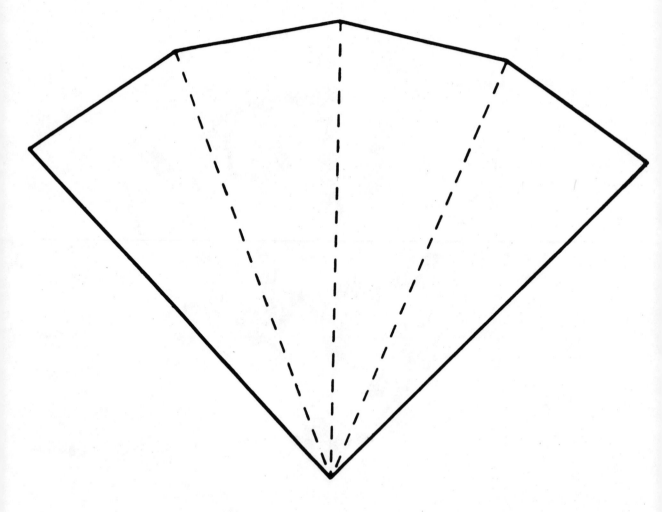

And so, once again, you find yourself staring stupidly at a Kryptec puzzle—huge gnats and flies buzzing around your ears, sun beating down, snakes sneaking about—while the fate of the whole expedition awaits your brilliant solution. During the pause, you briefly consider resigning from The Society and taking up a more sedate hobby like stamp collecting. But the wary glances of the others bring you back to the task at hand. Looking carefully at the paper, you notice that it had once been folded along the lines radiating from its point. One by one, you recrease them, folding each one in the same direction until you have formed the piece of paper into a tall thin pyramid with four sides. This strikes you as a rather neat discovery. You look up. Pancho, drinking water from a canteen, gives you a quizzical glance. Ace turns expectantly toward you. Dr. Dentons raises a hopeful eyebrow. You smile weakly but there's nothing to tell, so you return to the pyramid. Somewhere on it is the secret image of the god Mixmox but you can't see it. You turn it, tilt it, tip it—but to no avail.

Where is the image, you wonder louder than you intended.

 Cut out the shape on page 101 along the solid lines, fold along the dotted lines, then tape the sides together to form a pyramid.

When you are just about ready to give up, you stand to stretch your legs and in so doing, gaze down at the pyramid from above. From this new perspective, the face of the god Mixmox jumps out at you, plain as the nose on your face.

"Eureka!" you shout. The others come running. You point down at the top of the pyramid, and each of them in turn gets to look into the serene face of Mixmox.

"See," you say, "it's the bird's-eye view that does it."

"Bird-brain's view," Ace says clearly reaching the limit of her patience. "Okay . . . so there's Mixmox and there's his mouth. Now what do we do about it?"

"You know, I think I remember seeing that face somewhere in the lost city," you say trying to place the memory.

Silence reigns as you try to decide what to do next. Take your paltry collection of prizes back to Big Mac? Return to the lost city? Beat a hasty retreat? Or stay for another round of darts?

7

Black Blood

Pancho has spent the morning sitting on the ground, morosely examining the Gold Jaguar medallion. The sadness of those who have lost a treasure they never possessed creeps across his face. Bored with the cheap idol, he casually flings it like a small frisbee in the direction of his knapsack. En route, the wind catches it, flips it sideways and sends it careening into a rock, where it easily breaks into five pieces.

"Oops," Pancho exclaims.

On further examination, however, the breaks do not seem to have been random.

"The medallion was made with slight indentations along these cracks," Dr. Dentons says after scrutinizing the pieces under his magnifier. "Look at how well-shaped they are, as though they were designed to break in just this way. Didn't you say there was some kind of depression in that rock where you found the medallion?"

"Yes," you answer, "there was a square indentation. Why?"

"I've got a crazy hunch. Maybe I'm just starting to understand the Kryptec mind. I have this feeling that if you were to rearrange these pieces into a square, they would fit neatly into that square indentation in the rock. What do you think?"

"What would that accomplish?" you ask.

"Who knows? Maybe the walls will move, or the floor will

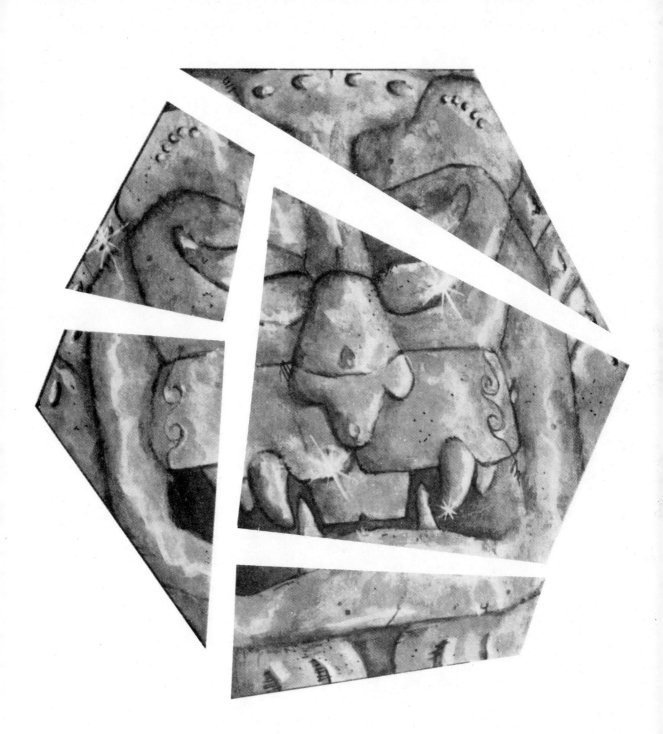

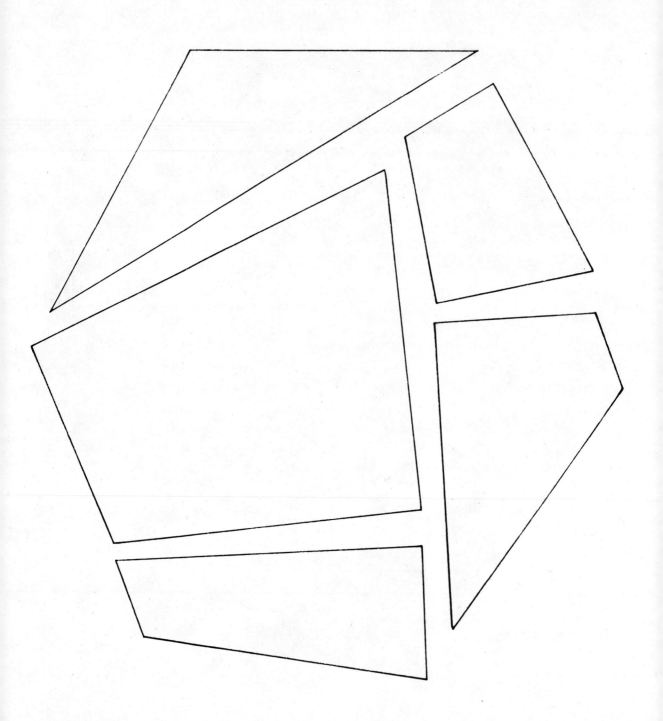

part or the heavens will rejoice. You never know around here. Like Pancho says, one thing's certain in Tortilla and that's that nothing's certain."

"The Kryptecs say that, Doc," Pancho explains. "I say let's get out of here while the getting's good."

"We can't do that, Pancho," Dentons replies, "we haven't found out all there is to know about the lost city. It still holds some secrets, I'm sure of it."

"Yeah, like when the assassins are going to get to assassinate *us!*"

"No, Paul's right," Ace says, "we can't leave until we explore every possible lead. Why don't you try rearranging those pieces? I think there's more to all this than meets the eye. I think soldiers working for the generals have taken over Pixtox for strategic reasons..."

"That would explain the phone booth," Dentons says. "It could be part of some sort of communications network in the jungle."

"No, Ace," Pancho says, wiping the anxiety from his brow, "if anything, it's Manero who's trying to kill us and make it look like the Kryptecs did it. Maybe this medallion is the last puzzle that leads to the real Gold Jaguar inside the lost city...the one with diamond eyes and ruby claws."

All eyes turn hopefully in your direction as you set to work. You turn the pieces this way and that, then this way again and try to form them into a square. It does indeed seem like it should work, but the nagging question is, as always, will it work for you?

Cut out the five shapes on page 105 and try to rearrange them into a square.

After much fiddling, you have the solution. Holding the triangular piece with its long base facing you, the other pieces fall in around it to form a perfect square. You show the jigsaw to the others.

"As I suspected," Dentons says. "We've got to return to Pixtox and set these pieces into that indentation in the rock. Something is bound to happen."

"Yes, but will it be good for our health?"

"One of us is going to have to stay here and guard the boats. We can't let anything happen to them or our escape will be cut off. I have a feeling that if Joe Chemilko knows where we are, so does all of Tortilla."

"That's a good idea, Ace, but logically I'm the one who should stay," Dentons says. "I'll just slow everyone down if my leg starts acting up."

"All right, Paul, that makes sense. You stay here and the three of us will go back to Pixtox. It shouldn't take us more than four or five hours. Let's break camp and pack up the boats, just in case we need to make a quick exit."

Once the *caballitos* have been loaded, Dr. Dentons takes a position sitting on a log, his rifle leaning on his shoulder, looking like a weekend sailor who has lost the wind. He lights his pipe, adjusts his glasses, sighs deeply and waves goodbye. As you leave, you see him framed by a clearing in the bush, lonely as a lizard...the perfect target.

Arriving at the west temple, you stop briefly to catch your breath. Pancho is leaning against one of the huge stones on the side of the steps when his hand suddenly slips and he goes tumbling to the ground. You help him get up and then discover the cause of the accident. An image has been painted on the rock with a greasy black substance which Pancho wipes off his hand with a handkerchief.

It is a familiar, frightening image that has been drawn recently.

"That's a bad sign, amigos."

"Why? What does it mean?"

"It's the sign of, you know, death. It's an ancient Indian symbol. The Spanish pirates stole it for their mast flags, and doctors stole it from them to denote poison. But for us the sign means we don't have much time."

"Come on, Pancho, you don't believe all this superstitious hoodoo..."

Whack! Whack whack!! Darts race through the air, bouncing off the rocks. They seem to be coming from all directions. The three of you take positions behind the west temple, ducking and weaving as you run. Once behind the cover of the stone wall, Ace returns the fire. The ground behind you slopes down and the thick foliage prevents the attackers from coming in that direction. You are momentarily safe.

"Look," Ace says to you with that familiar expression of firm panic, "Pancho and I will hold them off. You're on your own."

"What? Me?"

"Yes, you! You're the only one who knows your way around in there. Get back to Pixtox and do what Paul said with the pieces of the medallion. We won't do you any good anyway," she says hastily reloading her rifle.

"How about guarding my rear?"

"That's what we *are* doing!"

"But I don't know if I can remember my way through the maze," you whine as you throw a coil of rope over your shoulder.

"Look for the mouth of Mixmox," Pancho suggests as he watches darts whizz by. "Then, when you find it, step into it. Maybe it's a secret passage! How thrilling! Whoops...Hey, that was close!"

"There's no time to argue. Get going!"

"See you soon, amigo...*Si Dios quiere.*"

"We'll wait for you here. If we can't hold this position, we'll try to lead them away and meet you back at the boats. *Hurry!*"

With her final words she gives you a good solid shove down the slope. You stop your downward slide by grabbing a branch, just as a wayward dart strikes a nearby bush. You bolt through the space between two huge vines and race back to the lost city. Monkeys laugh, macaws caw, beetles chirp, but you pay no attention. Soon the great stone walls rise before you. You enter through the left gate and start searching desperately for the face of the god Mixmox, the face drawn on the paper pyramid, that will lead you on your fateful return to the jaguar's chamber.

Return to the maze on pages 88–89 and try to find the face of Mixmox.

After a few false starts, you find the idol right near the gate, alone in a courtyard. The mouth of the monolith is an open hole that is just big enough for you to crawl into. Inside, you find that the statue is hollow and below it is a long tunnel that runs straight ahead. Trying to ignore your

natural fears of the dark, of bugs, strange tunnels, angry gods and all, you run through the subterranean tube. Shells crunch beneath your feet, webs slither across your skin, humming wings flap in your face, but you press on and emerge—minutes later— behind the stele in the court before the tower with three doors. It has been a shortcut through the maze, just as Pancho predicted. Up the steps, through the middle door, past the hidden doorway, down the chute and—breathless and tingling— you are back in the secret chamber. The rock is still there on the ground, untouched, unmoved.

You put down the rope, prop the flashlight on your shoulder and take out the five pieces of the puzzle. One by one you assemble them into the square indentation. They fit perfectly. You step back and wait. But nothing happens. The only sound you hear is the racing throb of your own heartbeat. Trying to catch your breath, you sit down on the rock—right on top of the medallion—and breathe slowly. When you are no longer gasping for air, you start to get up but the motion of your heels digging into the dirt floor impels the rock backward. The whole stone, as if on a track, slides two feet to the rear with you riding on it. Looking down between your legs, where the rock formerly stood, there is now a large hole approximately two feet square. The rock had covered it completely.

You shine your light and peer down into the opening. There is clearly another room below the one you are sitting in. The hole in the floor of your chamber is an opening in the ceiling of the room below. There is a low humming sound filtering up through the hole.

You want to bolt out into the sunlight, but know that you are being paid—and paid well—to climb down and investigate. Moments pass as you weigh the risks. Then, muttering and griping, you uncoil the rope, tie one end around the rock and drop the other end down the hole. Then, hand under hand, you lower yourself down.

The rope is short; it ends a few feet from the bottom but how far you cannot tell. You dangle. Then, committing yourself to the puzzle world, you let go and fall three or four feet. Your thud echoes coolly in the cavern. You flip on your flashlight and look around. This lower chamber is larger than the one above, colder, and filled with a familiar aroma that you can't quite place. In the middle of the room you are confronted with a very bizarre sight indeed.

There stands a large mechanism of some kind, about the size
of an elevator, humming with energy. It is a complicated
arrangement of pipes, valves and meters and resembles a big, fat
Tinkertoy set. The largest pipe—about a foot in diameter—rises
straight out of the ground then makes a sharp turn and runs
horizontally for about ten feet until it plunges into the cave wall.
All the other pipes, wheels and joints are clustered around it. At
its foot there is a computer terminal with a telephone
attachment.

You have no idea what this discovery is but you know for sure
that it isn't made of gold, isn't a primitive artifact and doesn't
resemble a jaguar. You make a quick sketch of it in your pad
while trying to pin down the thick odor that fills the room. You
finally give up, decide you've done all you can and prepare to
leave. Making sure that your Cracker Jack, flashlight, pad and
pencil are secure, you grab the rope which is dangling at chest
height and start to climb.

But there is a problem. Although sliding down the rope was a
snap, climbing up is quite impossible. The rope is too thin. The
weight of your body makes it sway and shake as you place one
hand over the other. You keep losing your grip. You try to climb
slowly without swinging, you try using your feet to steady the
rope, twisting it around your leg...but each time you reach
upward, the rope jiggles and you slip to the floor.

It soon becomes clear that the only way to succeed is to secure
the lower end of the rope. That would keep it taut and stabilize
it but its lower end is hanging four feet from the cavern floor
and the builders haven't put a hook on the ground for your
benefit.

A quick calculation tells you that no combination of socks, shorts and shirt will make a good extension for the rope. You curse yourself for not wearing a belt or boots with laces.

You look around frantically. There is a chain hanging from one of the pipes of the apparatus. Perfect, you say, maybe the builders *did* have you in mind. You grab the loose end of the chain and walk toward the rope... but it won't reach. Then you lay the chain out as far as it can go and try to grab it while holding the end of the rope. Again, no luck. Your hand is still two feet away. You try swinging the rope and you do get closer but it is too thin and won't sway steadily. What do you do?

You check your possessions... pad, pencil, flashlight, gun. But wrapping, scribbling on, illuminating or shooting the rope won't do any good. It is while bouncing the gun in your hand that the solution comes to you. When is a gun not a gun, you ask yourself in bogus Kryptec. The answer to that question proves to be your key to freedom.

In a few moments the rope is tied to the chain and you start to climb. It still isn't easy but the tension on the lower end allows you to go up, scamper through the hole in the ceiling and crawl back into the upper chamber. There you untie the rope, drop it down into the hole and push the rock back into position. Then it's back to the surface, down the steps of the tower, into the secret tunnel and—in less time than you thought—you are crawling out of the mouth of Mixmox in the courtyard near the front gates.

Just as you are leaving the city and saying your final good riddance, you hear voices. You duck behind one of the walls in time to see two men racing into the first court. They are carrying rifles and large spotlights and one of them is carrying a rope ladder over his shoulder. They run directly to the statue of Mixmox and climb into the mouth. When they are gone, you come out of hiding, check the bush for others, look around in all

directions, take a deep breath...and hightail it into the jungle.

Grabbing feverishly at roots and stumps, you charge back up the hill behind the west temple, only to find that your companions are gone. The whole area is deserted. The ground where you last saw Ace and Pancho is covered with darts and spent rifle shells. You decide to go on to the boats and discover that, as a novice in the jungle, your terror is a fine navigator. Without stopping to wonder where you are headed, you thrash your way through the thick and soon find yourself at the clearing where the boats had been tied. But there is no one there either, the supplies are gone and only one boat remains. Where have the others gone? Are they waiting for you down river at the plane? Or have they been captured? Should you look for them?

Just then you hear shouts and the sounds of people coming your way in a hurry. You start to call out Pancho's name but catch yourself in time. It is a group of armed men, shouting in English about not letting you get away. Something about their brash manner tells you not to stick around for a chat. You jump into the remaining boat, push off from the shore, duck down and let the river current carry you away.

After drifting a few hundred yards beyond the clearing, you peek out from behind the upturned stern of the canoe. Luckily, the gang has not noticed the boat. You stand up, take your pole in hand and start to help the river's current. It is then that you notice a figure at the shoreline. It is the old Indian...Joe Chemilko. He is sitting in his chair, smoking one of his thick cigarettes. He is beckoning you, signaling you to come closer. "Is it safe?" you wonder out loud. Does he know where Ace and Pancho and Dr. Dentons are? Or is it a trap? Can you trust him or are you better off trying to get out of Tortilla by yourself right now?

 If you decide to head the boat over to Joe Chemilko, read on. If you decide to pass him by and return to the plane, turn to page 118.

You lean hard to the left side of the boat, push down on the pole and veer toward shore. It is a fight against the downstream force of the current but you eventually get the boat pointing directly at the old man. By the time you reach the bank and pull the canoe up onto a rock, he has already gotten up from his chair and is walking into the jungle. You follow. For someone almost as old as Cortez, he does a fine job of brisk tropical hiking. It's hard to keep up with him as he forges ahead intently, as if he had memorized every root and twig in his path.

Soon you arrive at a group of huts, the usual Kryptec design of branches and leaves. Joe turns to you, smiles a toothless smile and points to the door of one of them. You walk inside, too tired to resist, and fully expect to find Manero and his herd ready to chain you and sell you into slavery.

"Well, well," Pancho says jumping up, "he really did find you, just like he said he would!"

Backs are patted, hands are shaken, hugs exchanged, hair is tousled. Everyone seems to be all right.

"Sorry we couldn't wait for you at the temple," Ace explains, "but we couldn't hold out any longer. The whole place is crawling with assassins. And they had traded in their darts for guns!"

"I know. I saw five more of them back at the river, all loaded up and ready to shoot. How many do you think there are all together?"

"Don't know, maybe ten."

"And why have they taken up this strange hobby of trying to kill us?"

"That all depends on what you found in Pixtox. What *did* you find?"

You tell your tale. You show your sketch. But before you can sit down and work out the details of your discovery, Ace interrupts the discussion.

"Listen, we can figure out all this later. The first thing we have to do is get out of here alive. If we don't hurry back to the plane, our murderous friends may get there first and then we're sunk. Pancho, show the brain the puzzle."

"Oh no," you groan.

"Oh yes," Pancho says as he takes out another of the paper puzzles and hands it to you. "It's another one of their *tlat*—you know, their sacred paper puzzles. Joe says he can lead us to safety and back to our plane but only if you can figure out this *tlat.*"

"What's the deal *this* time?"

"This one's called Macuilzochitl's Revenge."

CUT OUT

TO ASSEMBLE

Cut out all three pieces on this page around their heavy black borders. On the large piece, also cut along the two vertical slits and cut out and remove the small rectangle below them.

Mount the two square pieces on heavy cardboard. Then, with all the pieces facing you, thread the end of the ribbon up through the rectangle from the back, into one of the slits, then out the other and back down through the open rectangle. Finally, glue or paste the loose square onto the free end of the ribbon. (The puzzle should now look like the diagram, with the square pieces on heavier cardboard.)

TO SOLVE

Can you separate the ribbon from the large piece without cutting or tearing any of the pieces?

"Swell," you say rubbing your temples and trying to stave off an impending headache.

"Yeah. Joe gave me some jazz about a myth in which our old friend Macuilzochitl has been imprisoned and has to escape or something. To tell you the truth, I couldn't follow it. The point is, you've got to separate these two pieces of paper without cutting or tearing them in any way. Kapeesh? He won't help us unless it's solved."

"That old coot!"

"Forget it. He's Kryptec, he means it."

"What does the word *tlat* mean anyway... torture?"

"No, it literally means something that you hold in your hand, grasp with your heart and solve with your mind. Sometimes they use the word to mean reality."

"Great."

There you are once more, staring down at a new puzzle, the solution of which is in your hands along with the fate of the expedition, the lives of your friends and probably of the entire planet as well. At this moment, the future of mankind seems to rest on your ability to separate two pieces of paper without cutting or tearing them. "And why not," you say trying to talk yourself into the task, "the future of mankind has to rest on *something*."

 Follow the instructions on page 115.

A quick fold, tuck and pull later, you are marching behind Joe's nephew on a trail near the river. You arrive back at Bimbo in the late afternoon to find that news of the day's events has already reached the village but the assassins themselves have not. The Indians are frightened. Rumors are spreading that Pixtox has been violated, that the assassins have failed to protect it and that the jaguar god is angry enough now to take a big bite out of Tortilla. A perfect time to end the vacation, Pancho suggests.

Before making your next move, you stake out the plane for a while, surveying the area to make sure it's safe. When the time is right, you quickly pack up Bimbo and take to the skies. From this aerial perch, you imagine that the jungle below is crawling with raging assassins.

In fifteen minutes, you make another jumpy landing at the airstrip near Hojos. None of the dismal news has reached this sleepy hamlet. The bus driver, the same dull-witted fellow who drove you to Hojos on the first day, has to be shaken from a deep five-day slumber. Soon you are jolting and bouncing your way to the border of Tortilla but it is only when you are on board the twin-engine plane that will take you to Mexico that you realize you have escaped the clutches of the jaguar.

Turn to page 120.

"No," you murmur, "he can't be trusted."

Something about Joe Chemilko's silent movements as he stands by the edge of the water seems suspicious. You pole harder down the river, trying to avoid fallen trees, low-hanging vines and curious alligators. You watch his antique form fading into the distance. By the late afternoon, you have been drifting down the Oozo for miles and begin to scan the trees looking for the plane. Finally, after almost giving up and preparing to drift forever, you spot the tail of Bimbo through an opening in the bush as the low sun twinkles off the metal. You pole over to shore, climb up the embankment and race over to pat Bimbo on the rump.

You climb into the cockpit and look around the landing strip but there is no sign of anyone, friend or foe. Not knowing quite what to do next, you sit at the controls, bite your fingernails and hope for inspiration.

Gunfire. Before you can scramble out of the front seat, Pancho and Dr. Dentons have opened the side door and shoved Ace's limp body onto the plane. Panting and gasping—and without any of their packs or supplies—they dive into the plane and slam the door. Outside, the stinging sounds of bullets zip by. Pancho points out the window and, following his finger with your gaze, you can see a band of men running toward Bimbo, shooting. Dr. Dentons is trying to revive Ace before the men come within bull's eye distance. Ace begins to moan and flail her arms but you can tell that by the time she regains consciousness, Bimbo will be target practice for beginners. If you could only take off! Get out of range until she wakes up! There were five steps... *only five*. But what were they? You *must* remember them... and quickly! What were the five simple steps for taking off?

Yes, that's it. The engine starts and the plane moves down the runway. When you reach the end of the strip, you turn around, head for the hunters and then, as if lifted by an unseen hand, Bimbo leaves the earth and shoots for the clouds.

By the time you manage to level out the flight path, Ace has recovered enough to take control again.

"What happened?" she asks shaking her head.

"You conked your head on a rock. Are you okay?"

"I'm fine. How did we get airborne?" she asks slipping into the pilot's seat and grasping the wheel.

You smile coyly and relinquish the controls. Not a moment too soon, she points out, since you have been heading in exactly the wrong direction over the Gulf of Mexico. Now, under her steady hand, you fly for twenty minutes then make another bumpy landing at the airstrip near Hojos. From there you take a jittery bus ride to the Tortillan border and, not soon enough, the twin-engine flight to Mexico and safety.

Turn to page 120.

"OIL!" Mac is shouting as he scans your report and studies the sketch you made. "This whole thing has been about oil!"

"Just as I suspected," Dr. Dentons says from the corner of the darkened room.

"Oil?" Pancho asks, screwing his face into one big wrinkle, "salad or hair?"

"Petroleum, Sanza, black gold. This contraption you've found is called a Christmas tree."

"Christmas tree? How festive!"

"Not that kind of tree, Pancho. This kind of Christmas tree is used to cap off an oil well. In certain types of oil wells there is enough pressure on the oil from the surrounding natural gas so that it doesn't need to be pumped out. Once the hole is dug, all you have to do is control the flow. That's the purpose of this Christmas tree. All these valves and wheels control the flow of the oil. And this particular model is computerized; it's a state-of-the-art electronic micro-model. It's about a third of the size of the old industrial ones but it produces four times the amount of oil."

"But how did they build it beneath the lost city?" Ace asks.

"Well, it's not really beneath the city. If your descriptions are correct, the cavern that this well is in is actually at the base of the rear wall of the city. My guess is that whoever built it dug a big hole behind the wall, sunk the rig into the pit, then roofed it over creating a cavern. Afterward, they made the only entrance through those two chambers by digging up into the Temple of the Jaguar. Very sneaky."

"And the phone booth and the meter we found were part of a communications network for monitoring the well?" Dentons suggests.

"Exactly. And you only stumbled upon part of the operation, every bit of it designed to fit in and disappear into the local archeological ruins. In that way, if any of the local villagers saw them communicating on the intercoms or reading the meters or entering Pixtox, they would think it was all part of the jaguar cult."

"But who is *they*? Who built all this?"

"Aminco, of course."

"Aminco??"

"Sure. It has to be. They must have discovered oil during their survey. Instead of reporting their findings to the government, they constructed this whole secret operation to steal..."

"The blood of the jaguar!" you shout.

"Yeah, they really did have their fingers in it," Pancho grins, "and while they were siphoning off the oil, they gave the Kryptecs all that bogey-wogey about the jaguar god sending assassins to keep people away from Pixtox. They knew it was the only way to keep the Kryptecs in line."

"So that assassin I killed in the temple was an employee of Aminco?" Dentons says with a grimace.

"All of the assassins are. Including the one who drew that death symbol in oil to scare you and the one who appeared before the old man and posed as Macuilzochitl himself. They went to pretty great lengths to carry this thing off. But now that the cat is out of the bag, so to speak, I don't expect them to hang around in Tortilla for too long."

"And the Gold Jaguar medallion?"

"As you discovered, it was a key they used to get access to the oil rig. Only they knew how to use it. Anybody else who found the chamber would think it was just an old relic resting near a rock. And if it was taken, they could easily make others."

"Was there ever a real Gold Jaguar?" Pancho asks hopefully. "You know, one with ruby claws and diamond eyes?"

"I don't know, Pancho. Want to go back and find out?"

"No thanks, Mac, I think I'll take a break from treasure hunting for a while."

"Then the coded poem," Dentons says, "that started us on this whole thing must also have been made by the people from Aminco."

"Right," Mac answers. "My guess is that they translated the original into English so they could find their way to the secret chamber. They had to get in there to build an entrance to the oil rig. Then they must have encoded it to prevent anyone else from using it. Of course, they didn't count on our ingenuity," he concludes with a nod in your direction.

"Paul?" Ace calls to Dentons. "Did you know all along that oil was involved here?"

"I had a hunch. The meter, the scraps of paper that looked like some kind of rate flow chart, then the rig . . . it was starting to fit together. If you follow that pipeline from the rig it probably leads straight to the gulf. They could easily barrel the oil there and sell it."

"Seems like a lot of trouble to go to for some oil. How much was the whole operation worth?" Ace inquires.

"I can only give you a guess," Mac responds. "What we've got here is a state-of-the-art electronic micro-rig. It uses enhanced tertiary methods of carbon dioxide injection..."

"We all know *that,*" Pancho says with his tongue planted firmly in his cheek.

"It might produce 1,000 barrels a day. Crude oil sells for about $35 per barrel right now so that's...almost $13 million a year. And there might be other hidden rigs as well."

"Gee," Pancho muses, "the lost city really was hiding a gold mine, except that it wasn't a *gold* gold mine."

"What are we going to do next, Mac?"

"The Society will prepare a full report for Señor Mentira, the cabinet member from the Tortillan government who contacted us originally. Their government will then be able to move in and take over the well and protect it from falling into the hands of the generals. It should give them a good source of income and collateral on world markets. Looks like the four of you have just saved a good decent democracy. You found something even more valuable than the legendary Gold Jaguar. You are to be congratulated," Mac concludes as he stands up ceremoniously and shakes each hand in turn. "Your checks will be sent to you in the usual manner. You've earned them. Goodbye."

Outside, in front of the flickering neon sign in the motel window, cars are waiting to take you away. There is a slight drizzle. You are tired and pleased at the thought of sleeping in your own bedroom devoid of turkeys and gnats. You actually look forward to your morning cereal, your electric bills, the simple routines of ordinary life. You do feel a vague nostalgia for the silent Kryptecs and their orderly world of puzzles...but nothing that a good hot bath won't cure.

"Are you going back to Central America?" you ask Ace. Wearing a tailored gray dress, she now seems less like a bush pilot than a corporate executive.

"Sure am. It's my home and besides, I've got a business to run. Things there will settle down eventually, especially now that oil has been discovered in Tortilla. If you're ever down there again, look me up; I'll take you for a ride over the countryside," she says and steps quickly and gracefully into the limousine.

Pancho and Dr. Dentons get into a second car. It seems that their homecoming will have to wait. They're off on another expedition for The Society.

"Don't tell me you're going to find the *real* Gold Jaguar," you groan leaning into the car window.

"No, we're off to Peru this time. Somebody's killing off the last of the Incas or something. Mac didn't really explain too much about it. Want to come along?"

"No thanks, I think I'll retire for a few months. Take it easy. Rest on my laurels."

"Okay, amigo, it's your funeral. But I have a funny feeling we'll be seeing you sooner than you think. It's just a hunch. You never know when something unexpected will come along. Remember the Kryptec saying… 'Mankind sleeps until startled by a puzzle.' *Adios!*"

With that, both cars pull out of the gravel driveway and push through the driving rain.

The next few days merge into the usual pattern. The dull regularity begins to erase all traces of your recent brushes with death, the fateful puzzles of the Kryptecs and the mysteries of the previous week. As a final gesture to prove to yourself that you have fully accepted your return home, you take apart your Cracker Jack pistol and put it back in the drawer along with the other secret weapons of The Society.

Four days after your report to Mac, an envelope arrives from the phone company. According to the attached letter, there has been a mistake in your account due to a computer error. You have been overcharged. They ask you to excuse this inconvenience and enclosed is a refund for $150,000. They hope that this compensates for any difficulty their error has caused.

You think back over the expedition and decide that it does. But the problem now is how best to spend the money. A new car? A yacht? A vacation perhaps? A trip to a small tropical country on the Gulf of Mexico?

THE END?

Not if you decide to read through the morning paper, in which case turn to page 124.

BELIZE, Honduras, Dec. 6

A group of military leaders who lost power in San Tortilla to the democratic regime of Presidente Delsol has made a new bid for the control of that troubled country. In a press conference today, the spokesmen for the exiled generals said that a new influx of financing from foreign nationals has made possible a new offensive against the unsteady government of Tortilla.

Officials were unclea̶ about the e̶x̶ ̶ ̶ource of thei̶ ̶ ̶ ̶ ̶nd̶ ̶ ̶ ̶y st̶ ̶ ̶ ̶ ̶ ̶ ̶ate th̶ ̶

Observers in neighboring Mexico and Guatemala noted that the generals' forces had made advances not against the capital city of Joe Chemilko—which was well protected by government troops—but near the ruins of an ancient city known as Pixtox in the southwestern part of the country.

Military analysts in the area were hard pressed to explain this move by the generals except to say th̶ ̶ ̶

 What's going on here?

Solutions

8   Special meeting of The Society called next week. Big money. Bring weapon. Prepare to take journey.

27   Come to me
         when my tallest son
         will point the way
         at a temple's point;
         then step into
         the mouth of _____
         and come to my
         secret chamber.

34   A pound of gold, regardless of its shape, will always be worth more than a half pound of gold.

38   The trick in weaving this fabric is to make it seem crude, since the irregularity of the lines is an optical illusion. All the horizontal lines are in fact straight and parallel.

39   Pick up two diagonal corner stones. The remaining two stones can now be used to form the side of a new, larger square.

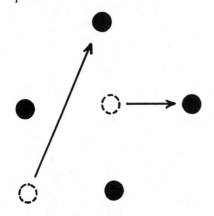

42

42   The answer is *chla*. First, break down the riddle into its three phrases. The first phrase is true ... *chla* is *not tlic* (they are different words) and therefore the answer is *chla*. This is the answer *unless* the second phrase is true; but the second phrase is false because *tlic* is *tlic* (they are the same word). Thus, the answer is still *chla* unless, as it states in the third phrase, the answer is *chla* ... in which case it's still *chla*.

44   The picture shows the ten digits and two symbols on the buttons of a push-button phone. Hardly a likely subject for an ancient Kryptec carving.

45   The answer is quite simple. The boy is her son.

46   Hold the egg *four* feet above the ground and let it drop. Although its shell has certainly broken, it has fallen *three* feet without breaking.

50   There is exactly the same amount of dirt in any hole of any size—namely, no dirt at all.

53 The difference is in the ring of animal heads. The quickest way to detect differences in pictures that are the same size (which is what you are trying to accomplish by holding one up in front of the other) is to flip the one in front. Differences in the design will flicker as if they were animated.

61 Assuming that Manero *always* cheated, Dr. Dentons reasoned that he had written the word "lose" on both pieces of paper. That way, Dentons would lose no matter which one he picked. To turn the tables, Dentons picked one at random and destroyed it before anyone had a chance to look at it. That forced Manero to reveal the remaining one, which of course had the word "lose" written on it and implied that Dentons had chosen the one with "win" written on it. Logic.

61 Clue #1 eliminates the downed plane and the great tree as possible sites, since you can't reach them by crossing exactly one bridge.

Clue #2 establishes that the clearing on the left is the one closest to the temples, since there are no paths from the other clearings that cross one or no

bridges. Since this clearing is close to the temples, they are obviously not near the stele.

Clue #3 eliminates the ruin, since the direction says you *pass by* it to get to the temples. The abandoned village is also eliminated, since the most direct route from either of the remaining clearings doesn't involve passing the ruin. There are now only two possible sites left...the lake and the sacred mound.

Clue #4 eliminates the lake, since there is no such path back to the camp. The temples are therefore near the sacred mound.

67 Make alternating cuts three-fourths of the way through the ring as shown in the diagram. You'll then be able to stretch the ring accordion-style and fit it over your head.

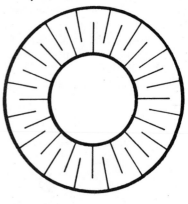

75 The panel on the right, three up from the bottom, has one less black space than any of the others.

77

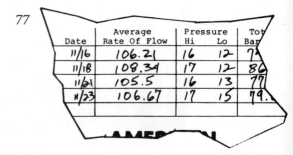

Date	Average Rate Of Flow	Pressure Hi	Lo	Tot Bar
11/16	106.21	16	12	7
11/18	108.34	17	12	86
11/21	105.5	16	13	77
N/23	106.67	17	15	79.

80   To see the image clearly, hold the page upright and position your eye at the right-hand border.

91

99

87

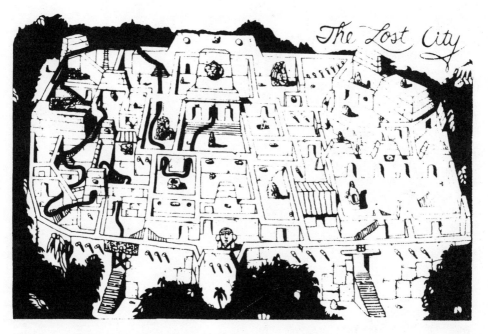

The Lost City

103

107

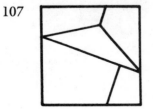

109 Go in through the left gate entrance, ascend, then descend.

112 Tie the gun (or you could also use your flashlight) to the bottom of the rope and use the added weight to swing it like a pendulum.

117 Take the band formed by the two slits, pull it forward and insert it through the rectangular opening. Pull it through the opening as far as you can and pull the ribbon through with it. You will now be able to slip the ribbon with its large squares out through the loop.

118 Ignition, throttle, brake, throttle and steer.

124 Mac and The Society have been tricked! Señor Mentira, the one-eyed visionary, apparently wasn't representing the government of San Tortilla at all. His presence at the press conference given by the generals (that's him with the eyepatch) indicates that he was working for them all along. He has turned over the information about the oil rigs to them and that has fueled their new advances in Tortilla. Your entire expedition has inadvertently helped to finance a new attempt at a right-wing coup. As the Kryptecs say…"The trickiest puzzle is the one you don't puzzle over."